Cultivating the Truth

Dorothy Dennehy Mystery Series, Volume 4

Jamie Tremain

Published by Jamie Tremain, 2023.

GENRE: Crime Fiction/Female Private Investigator/Police Procedure

Cultivating the Truth

A Dorothy Dennehy Mystery
Book #4
Copyright © Jamie Tremain
November 2023
FIRST EDITION

Cover Design: www.jennifergibson.ca[1]
For more information, contact jamietremainJT@yahoo.com

---

1. http://www.jennifergibson.ca

1

CHAPTER ONE

Rolin Montase stood behind the bar of Maxwell's Bar and Grill in Portland, Oregon. The tall, dark-complexioned Haitian was in his element, enjoying repartee with customers on busy Saturday. He flicked a towel over the well-worn bar surface as he dealt with a group of boaters from the marina. They jostled good-naturedly to find seating at the bar. Rolin pointed them over to a spot across the floor. "There's a table free in the corner."

As they moved away, he overheard, "See, I told you. He does look like LL Cool J, right?"

Rolin had heard it before, and it always amused him. As his eyes followed the boaters, his vision focused on his business partner, Dorothy Dennehy. She was sitting with, he assumed, a potential client for her investigation agency. Her body language sharpened his focus.

Although she recently handed over much of Quail International Investigations and Security to her right-hand man, HB, she liked to keep her skills sharp by taking an occasional case herself.

Rolin, an experienced criminal lawyer, paid close attention to her table companion.

His jacket and tie suggested he was a businessman, late forties. But he was agitated. His fist pounded the table, and he grew angrier and more animated by the second.

Rolin's hackles rose when he heard a loud and vocal threat directed at her. "You'll be sorry, lady, when this happens, and you did nothing to stop it." He tossed a card on the table. "Here's my number. You'll be calling!"

Rolin kept his cool and spoke to another employee. "Colleen, can you manage here for a few minutes? I need to circulate."

He picked up a tray, collected empty glasses, and chatted with regulars as he made his way to where Dorothy sat. He knew she could handle herself in most situations, and as a former cop she wouldn't be amused if she thought he was coming to her rescue. Rolin approached the table. "Can I get you two a refill?"

Dorothy stood abruptly, scraping her chair on the polished oak plank floors. Her green eyes flashed annoyance. "No, thank you, Rolin. This is Xander Michelson, and he is leaving - now."

Rolin followed her lead, as nearby patrons stared on curiously. Michelson stood up, his flushed face displaying his anger. An attractive man in his fifties he looked as if he worked out but was no match for Rolin's size and presence. Without another word, he stormed out of the premises.

Dorothy tossed her shoulder-length red hair in dismissal. "Whew, what an unpleasant character! If you can take a break, let's talk in your office where it's more private." Rolin tipped his head. "After you."

***

Dorothy led the way, greeting customers and assuring them all was good. Followed by Rolin, they headed for the back of the restaurant - to Rolin's dock-side legal clinic.

After she and Rolin had agreed to partner and take over running Maxwell's from her father, they'd converted a spacious area off the restaurant so that Rolin could also pursue his passion — providing legal assistance to the underprivileged and marginalized. He'd had his fill of international, high-profile cases. On the weekends he enjoyed the change of pace and atmosphere tending bar afforded him.

She stood aside as he unlocked the office door and led her to a pair of leather armchairs. The comfortably furnished room provided outside access for clients when needed. She continued to feel pleased at the arrangement they'd agreed upon when they'd bought the building from Maxwell Dennehy.

Rolin had been ready for a new chapter in his life, downsizing from both his prestigious international law practice, and downtown condo in Portland, in order to serve those who needed legal aid.

Together, they'd created this practical and functional office for him, and he'd been happy to take up residence in the modest apartment above. Rolin often told her it was the best of both worlds.

Rolin, who generally knew when to keep quiet, could hardly contain himself.

"He's a nasty one. Someone I should know about?"

She couldn't help but laugh at his consternation. "That'll teach me for trying to help out. HB's schedule meant he couldn't see this guy, so I offered. Some days, my friend, I get all the crazies. Xander Michelson wants me to look into a crime that's not even happened! And there's me without my crystal ball today. Nut job, right?"

His full lips curved in a smile. "I sense a story coming on. Would you like a glass of red to help?"

She laughed. "Yes please."

The two friends had developed a teasing banter that flowed naturally between them. She took the glass of red wine, crossed her long legs, and started with a toast.

"Cheers!" She raised her glass in Rolin's direction. After her first sip, she smiled. "Right, here's the irony. Xander Michelson, according to what he tells me, was a partner in a — wait for it — winery."

"Interesting. Local I assume?"

"Yes, but," Dorothy leaned over to examine the open wine bottle. "Not this winery, though. He was a partner in Michard Estates Winery and thinks his former partner is in great danger."

"Aha, now I see. Michard Estates is one of our suppliers , and one of the best Pinot Noirs in the area."

Dorothy tipped her glass back. "One of our best sellers as well, if I'm not mistaken. Anyway, when he contacted HB, he misled him into thinking it was a supply issue we needed to deal with. So, I wasn't prepared to take case notes."

"Wrong kind of case," Rolin winked at her.

She smiled and continued. "According to Michelson, he's heard rumors of a loose cannon type, I think his name is Frisco Butler, who is an employee at the winery. Says this Butler has a major grievance against his former business partner. A grievance which Michelson fears could put a life in danger. For now, it's a non-issue anyway, and because I didn't take any notes, I'm not wasting time fact-checking anything."

"You said former partner? I'm a little intrigued as to his intent, even if there is no basis for an investigation."

She frowned. "Yes, and that's thirty minutes spent listening to his rant I won't get back! I don't imagine I'm getting the full story as he was fuelled by anger. And, of course, only his side of things. What I do remember is this. His former partner is Etienne Rivard — now sole owner of Michard Estates — and they had a falling out. Michelson was vague on what happened, and the partnership was dissolved. I only half-listened. I told him I'm not in the prevention business and I couldn't help him."

"Here's a question for you, then. How did he learn about this supposed danger if he's no longer a partner? I'd assume he wouldn't be on the premises anymore."

"I questioned him on that as well. He says he reached out to Rivard last month and hoped enough time had passed that he would be welcome at a birthday party for Rivard's teenage daughter, Charlotte, this month. Who happens to be his goddaughter, as well."

"So Rivard must have relented, allowed his former partner to visit, and that's how Michelson learned about the threat?"

"I suppose." Dorothy finished her wine and stood. "I think your break is over, sir and we both need to get back to work." She made to leave Rolin's office. "Oh, by the way, Dad and Alanna invited us to join them here for dinner tonight. I'll put the reserved sign on their favorite table. Dad should get a laugh with this one. Another strange story he can add to the collection he's heard during his time with the police force."

She looked down at her friend, who hadn't moved from his comfy chair. Rolin appeared deep in thought. As if he hadn't heard her dinner invitation, he kept to the topic of the non-case. "So, what do you think he meant by 'in danger'? And why would he want to help his old partner when the partnership no longer exists?"

"Well, listen to you. You're starting to think like an investigator. If there's anything to this, and Michelson is legitimately concerned, I'd say it would be because of his goddaughter. He spoke about her with great affection. Good questions, but I don't have any real answers for you. Should I add you to the payroll?" Her mood darkened. "I don't like a situation where children could be at risk."

She forced a brighter tone to her voice. "Anyway, you can discuss this non-case with Dad tonight. I want to talk to Alanna about some decorating ideas she has for their in-law apartment at the house. Since they moved in it's been non-stop."

Rolin finally stood, picking up the empty wine glasses. "Max is sure to have some ideas on your new friend, so dinner sounds good. By the way, Dee, how are the new living arrangements working out?"

"To be honest I found it hard to have anyone else in Paul's and my space on a permanent basis. We were there for such a short time before ... the murder." She closed her eyes, pushing away the nightmare reminder.

"Sorry, it still hurts, doesn't it?"

She nodded and forced a smile on her face. "That's life. No guarantees. I'm grateful the house provided the option to have Dad, and Alanna close by, and it's manageable since the new addition to the back. Alanna, and I, need our own kitchens, don't you know."

"I understand perfectly. And never forget, as Paul's best friend, I will always remember him as the special person he was."

"Wasn't he though. I still feel his presence, and miss him every day, but it's getting better. Dad and Alanna, I hardly ever see as they keep to themselves or they're off gallivanting somewhere. They want to host a barbecue at their new home before the weather changes."

"Sounds like a plan. So, what's on the menu tonight?"

"Thanks for reminding me. I'd better check with the kitchen because Dad has requested fresh lobster!"

"Then I'll be there. One of my favorites. And I'd better get back to the bar or I'll have to apprentice as a P.I. for extra cash."

"Mr. Montase, it takes a special person to be a P.I. But I'll consider you for some nighttime surveillance duty if you think you're up for it."

Rolin smiled in amusement, "Hmm. See you at dinner."

***

"So why lobster, Dad? I can't believe your new diet would allow it .Lobster smothered in butter! You should be watching what you eat since the heart attack."

Max gave an exaggerated sigh. "Stop fussing darlin'. I get enough from Alanna. Sure, you can order what you like from the menu but we're having lobster and a bottle of bubbly as we are celebrating." The burly, sandy-haired Irishman had passed his stubbornness on to his daughter.

Saturday night and Maxwell's was crowded, even with the extra spacing between tables. They sat at the best seats in the house — perks of ownership — watching the sun fade into twilight across the river. Gently bobbing boats began to turn on their lights. Dorothy loved the magical air it lent to the scenery.

She thought her stepmother looked especially lovely. The former public relations queen, now in her mid-sixties, adored her father, which could be the reason for Alanna's relaxed manner. And yet, Dorothy picked up another current below the tranquil appearance. As if she held a secret dying to be revealed. Dorothy could wait and she took a moment to be grateful she and Alanna had become fast friends, both with Max's best interest at heart.

"Celebrating? Do tell. It's not your birthday so..."

Rolin laid his hand on Dorothy's. "Dee, let them tell us in their own time although, I admit wanting to know as well."

Dorothy watched Max try unsuccessfully to keep a huge smile off his face as he turned to Alanna. "Do you want to tell them, luv? I know you're bursting to do the honors."

Before Alanna could react, a server came to the table with a platter of appetizers, halting the conversation until he left. Dorothy sat on the edge of her seat. "Alanna, the suspense is killing me."

Alanna's blue eyes sparkled as she smiled benevolently at her husband. "Here we go. Everyone knows the pandemic impacted all kinds of travel, and now it's so exciting to finally have things open up. Max and I considered all sorts of places to spend our hard-earned money, but we settled on this one trip."

"And?... Where are you going? A tour of Britain? Ireland, then to visit the birthplace of the Dennehy's? No, it's Italy, I'll bet." Dorothy knew travel-loving Alanna had a long bucket list.

"No none of the above. Max has booked us a trip to Alaska on a cruise ship. We'll travel the Inside Passage, relax and see a new part of the world. One more to score off my list."

While Dorothy searched for the right way to frame her concerns, it would have taken a pin dropping to break the silence.

"But do you feel it's safe? Aren't there still issues with cruises? You're not getting any younger Dad, and your health ..."

"Darlin', you just said the magic words. I'm not getting any younger, so I need to seize the day. It's not until next May, almost eight months away, when the weather should be favorable, but in the meantime, I'm still free to work in the bar if you need me."

She knew she'd never win the argument with her father. "You know I count on you to show up regularly. You've a lot of customers here who still see you as the face of Maxwell's. Just make sure your travel insurance covers another wave - and I'm not talking water!"

Dinner arrived along with a bottle of champagne. Rolin, with Dorothy's permission, told them about her run-in with Xander Michelson and his strange request.

Max perked up when he heard the name Michard Estates. "They're one of our biggest suppliers. Or I should say, yours now. Carry some of the best wines in the region."

Max shook his head over the story Rolin shared.

"I'd heard the partnership had broken up. Some rumors about a marriage on the rocks with Rivard and his wife, Olivia St John-Rivard, but what a strange story. In all my years as a cop and helping Dorothy with private investigations I've never had a case to work on that hadn't happened!" Max tried to continue the fun with his daughter, asking if he'd still be paid to work on a case set in the future.

But neither Dorothy nor Alanna paid attention. They were deep in conversation about paint colors and drapery fabrics while they waited on dessert. Max and Rolin shared a shrug of commiseration.

They'd settled with dessert and coffee when a small-statured man, full of nervous energy, approached. His well-worn face made him look older than his years, testament to a hard-lived life. HB — Holden Bartholemew — coughed softly.

"Boss, sorry, I didn't know you'd be having a family dinner."

"HB, lad," boomed Max. "Pull up a chair. You're as good as family, too, you know."

HB, a man of few words, had a special bond with Max, going back more than two decades. Dorothy had made him her top agent in her early days of being a private investigator. He now lived on Dorothy's houseboat, *The Private, Aye?* which doubled as the office and operations center for Quail International.

"Yes, HB. Join us, please. You must be here for a reason." Dorothy pulled in a chair from the next table and the four diners adjusted their places to make room.

He hesitated but gave in to being outnumbered. He sat, and removed his ball cap, revealing a nest of still-dark curls beneath. "It's nothing that couldn't wait, boss. Some paperwork and expense reports to be signed. I thought you'd be working behind the bar, not having dinner."

"Hand it over." Dorothy pushed her plate aside and took the file from HB. Knowing she could trust his eye for detail meant she quickly signed where needed. But it was the last expense report, with the fluorescent yellow sticky that made her look at HB, her pen poised in mid-air.

"Aha - this is what you wanted me to see, isn't it?"

HB nodded. "We might have a problem with the expenses Jordan's claiming."

"I'll say. Why would he need three boxes of ammo, for a gun he's not licensed to carry?"

Max pulled the invoice toward him. "HB, son, I think you and I should have a wee chat with Jordan. Sooner rather than later."

CHAPTER TWO

Jordan Klein, a thirty-something operative employed by Quail International, sat across from grim-faced HB and laid-back Max. His long and limp dirty-blond hair was pulled back. They sat at a corner table in Maxwell's. Dorothy's rule about limiting visits to the *Aye* was set in stone. HB agreed. He valued his privacy, too.

Max had turned the expense report around in order for Jordan to see it. Among charges listed for fuel and fast food was a one-line item, highlighted for clear visibility. In case Jordan wasn't sure, Max pointed a finger to the offending line.

"Now then, boyo, I'd like for you to explain to your boss here, and me, just what you'd be needing 12-gauge shells for. I don't recall Dorothy making changes to the 9mm handguns she allows her team to carry?"

Jordan shifted in his chair, avoiding eye contact with either of them.

HB's tone was harsher than Max's. If Jordan was a problem, it was his screw-up to fix. The duties Dorothy had bestowed upon him included new hires, and Jordan had been his first experience. Had he blown it? "You're still on three months' probation with us, so if this job means anything to you, don't mess it up."

"Listen, lad. We all make mistakes, but if you want to keep working for HB, and my daughter, we need to know you're someone to be trusted. Got it?"

Jordan's head bobbed, and he pushed the paper away. "I'm sorry. I was going to pay it back. I - I bought the ammo for my cousin..."

"You what!" HB shot to his feet. "What the hell, man. Did you think we wouldn't notice this? I'm the one who dispenses the gun supplies. We wouldn't use a single box of ammo in a year between all of us, and you ordered three! These are for shotguns! I'm waiting!"

Jordan scratched the side of his head, swallowed hard, and bounced his gaze between the intimidating men in front of him. "Okay, okay. My cousin knows I can get some things wholesale because of work, and when he asked if I could get shotgun shells for him — he hunts deer — I agreed. He lives off grid, see. Feeds his family from his own garden and the occasional deer. Not much money, so ..."

Max raised an eyebrow, but HB jumped right in. "And this cousin. What's his name and where can I find him? You'd think me a dumbass investigator if I didn't check your story, right?"

***

Across the floor of the restaurant, Dorothy stood behind the bar, Rolin at her side as they checked invoices and inventory totals. They couldn't hear the meeting between the three men, but when Dorothy had seen HB jump to his feet, she nudged Rolin. "I'll get the full story from Dad, but judging by the shocked face on poor Jordan, I believe HB has made his point."

The meeting had been arranged before the restaurant opened for the lunch hour, so there were no patrons. Dorothy crooked a finger at Colleen, who was setting tables. She put her bundle of cutlery down and came over. "Yes?"

"Go over to my dad's table and ask if they want anything. I think their meeting is about to break up."

Colleen returned with a request for two beers. "The young guy is leaving."

"Bet he can't wait to get out of here," Rolin commented.

To her surprise, when Jordan got up from the table, he didn't move to the exit, but came in their direction.

"Ms. Dennehy. We haven't officially met, but I know you're HB's boss. He hired me a few weeks ago, and I screwed up. I just want you to know, I'm sorry and it won't happen again." He held out his hand to shake and quickly retracted it. "Sorry. Keep forgetting these aren't a good idea anymore."

Not in a million years would Dorothy have predicted this scene. Stunned, she hoped her face didn't show her surprise. "Jordan, right? Listen, I appreciate your honesty and I trust HB's experience. If he hired you, he sees potential. A lesson learned today I think?"

Jordan nodded. "Yes ma'am."

She cringed at the moniker, but it seemed sincere, and she let it pass. "Can I get you a drink, something to eat?"

"Thanks anyway, but I need to go. See you around."

"Yes, you will. Take care, Jordan."

Max and HB had hung back, but now came forward to take their bottles of beer at the bar, giving Dorothy and Rolin a rundown.

"Boss, you never told me hiring people could backfire."

Max patted HB on the shoulder. "Now then, my son, life is a learning experience, is it not? I think, between the two of us just now, we've put young Jordan on the right path. And if I'm any judge of character at all, I'd say the lad will not be making similar mistakes in the future."

"I agree with Dad's assessment, HB. But I'm sure you'd rather be on night surveillance with a full bladder than deal with employee issues."

"Maybe. But I'm still checking out the cousin."

"We'd be disappointed if you didn't," concluded Rolin. "Drink up men, doors will open in fifteen, and Dee and I still have work to do. Unless you want to pay for those brews?"

***

The skies had let loose with a torrential autumn downpour when two days later, HB met Dorothy at the bar. He confirmed Jordan's cousin-story had checked out. And Jordan had repaid the expense item in full.

"And we all know about second chances, don't we HB?"

"Point taken, Boss. Jordan can stay, for now, but I'll be keeping my eye on him, don't worry."

"I know you will. Anything new I should know about? I heard the missing laptop case has been resolved?"

HB handed over a printed page. "Here's this week's summary. Three cases closed, one ongoing, and two requests I have to check to see if they're worthwhile taking on." He looked at his boss, and friend, as she bent her head to read.

When her fiancé, Paul, had been killed, he felt they'd grown closer. An even stronger friendship, and while he harbored deeper feelings for more, he knew it could never be. He'd lost the love of his life, Emily, decades ago. He and

Dorothy shared that in common. Losing a soul mate and knowing the void would never be filled. He mentally kicked himself. How was it he could recognize these emotions in his mind, but could never find the words to say them aloud?

"Sorry, Boss, what did you say?"

"You were miles away, my friend. I asked whether you'd be assigning Jordan to either of these new cases."

"Thinking about it." His attention went to the doorway of the storeroom located behind the bar. "I think Rolin wants you." He pointed behind her, where Rolin had emerged, an expression he couldn't quite peg etched on his face.

"You need to hear this, Dee."

***

Dorothy sent HB on his way with an admonition to remember his umbrella and then turned her attention to Rolin. "What's up?"

"One of the delivery drivers. C'mon."

The well-stocked storeroom opened to the receiving area for Maxwell's. The open door reminded Dorothy of standing beneath Niagara Falls; sheets of water blocking any view to the outside world. She watched as a sodden delivery person ducked through the downpour with a case of wine which he stacked atop two others stamped Michard Estates Winery.

"Hey, buddy. Over here for a minute, okay?" Rolin had to raise his voice over the deafening rain.

"Glad to if it means I don't have to go back out in that!"

Rolin nodded. "We haven't had a deluge like this in some time. I think I saw the Ark float by an hour ago."

They chuckled and Dorothy waited on Rolin's lead. "This is Dorothy Dennehy. She and I are co-owners of this place. She'll be interested to hear what you told me a few minutes ago."

The driver frowned. "About the winery?"

"Yes, your boss specifically."

Dorothy's radar twitched and she moved in closer to read the driver's name on his uniform jacket - Carter Hayes. She wished she had her notebook, sensing what she was about to hear might be noteworthy.

Carter hesitated. "Listen, I don't want to get in trouble, and some of this is only rumor."

"Go on," encouraged Dorothy.

"Well, I heard there was a big, physical, fight between my boss and another of the workers. Might have been Frisco, they butt heads all the time."

Dorothy recognized the appeal of drawing out a story when one is the center of attention, but this guy had it down pat. "And?"

"And now Etienne Rivard has disappeared. Gone, no notice. Nothing missing, just him. As if he disappeared off the planet."

CHAPTER THREE

"Sorry, Dorothy, Sergeant Pierson is on leave."

"When did that happen? Is he okay?" Dorothy had helpful contacts in the Portland Police Bureau but hadn't heard about Pierson. Must have been sudden for him to be away and not let her know.

"He'll be okay, personal leave for a couple of months. I can't really give you details; you know?"

"Of course. Pass along my best wishes if you're talking with him?"

"Roger that. I can put you over to his replacement if you like. It's Sergeant Shelby Keleher. She's up from Los Angeles. I think she's at her desk."

"Thanks." Dorothy had only a moment to wonder about the new sergeant in charge while the call was transferred. She thought back to Detective D'Amico and could only hope Keleher wasn't cut from the same cloth.

The phone connected. "Keleher. How can I help you?"

"Sergeant Keleher, Dorothy Dennehy here. I have a situation I'd like to discuss with you — later today if possible?"

"Dennehy?" Dorothy heard the sound of paper rustling. "Right, I knew I'd seen something. You run Quail Investigations, correct?"

"Yes, and I recently ..."

"I can see you now. Is that a problem?"

"No, I'll be there in 20 minutes."

The phone went dead in Dorothy's hand. Nope, she didn't think Keleher was another D'Amico. Whether that was a good thing, she'd have to wait to find out.

***

Keleher was on the phone when Dorothy arrived. The sergeant stood at her desk and alternated with pacing as far as the phone cord would allow. Blonde, almost as tall as Dorothy, and antsy. When she wasn't speaking, her lips were pursed, which highlighted her cheekbones. Dorothy thought she might be young for the job, but who was she to judge? Keleher pointed at the chair in front of her desk, and Dorothy sat.

She hadn't been to the station for a few months — mostly HB's territory now — but she wanted to see what Keleher thought of Xander Michelson's claim, now his boss had apparently disappeared.

"I'll want the details. The sooner the better." Keleher hung up, scribbled on the file in front of her and then closed it. She remained standing and looked down at her visitor.

"So, you're Dorothy Dennehy. I thought you were semi-retired by what I've heard around here."

And nice to meet you as well. "Emphasis on semi."

"Right. You have a murder to report? This is homicide and major crimes detail - not missing persons, or narcotics."

Dorothy liked to build a rapport with those she'd be working with, but this wasn't off to a good start. "I need to explain. Far as I know there isn't a major crime, or murder – yet."

"Go on."

Dorothy relayed her meeting with Xander Michelson, and then what she'd learned about Etienne Rivard's possible disappearance. "So, I wondered if you've heard anything concerning Mr. Rivard. Or if Frisco Butler has ever been on your radar."

"No, sorry. Means nothing to me, but I'll note it for future reference. So, if that's all?" Keleher remained standing, and Dorothy knew her time was up.

She rose and repositioned her shoulder bag. "If you do hear anything, can you let me know? For my own records, you understand."

"It will depend on what I hear. Thank you for coming in."

And then she picked up her phone once again and punched in a number. Dorothy was no stranger to being ignored, but this was a 5-star act.

She turned and passed by Ted Jellico's desk - just outside Keleher's office. She'd worked with Ted in the past and nodded a greeting. She thought he was going to say something, but changed his mind, and only received a reciprocal nod.

The atmosphere in the division was subdued. Everyone focused on work, with heads down. She'd bet the team missed the easy-going manner of Reg Pierson. She'd be glad when he returned, too.

Driving back to the marina and Maxwell's, she puzzled over the mood of the homicide department and the distinct chill she'd received from Shelby Keleher. She'd have to ask HB for his take on her if they'd met yet. But what to make of the possible disappearance of Rivard? Was something going on that Michelson had warned her about?

Her musings were interrupted by an incoming call. She chose the hands-free option to answer.

"Dorothy? Ted. I only have a minute, and this is off the record, okay?"

"Sure Ted, go ahead."

"The new boss, Keleher. By the book all the way – no information to be given to outsiders. And she'd kill me if she knew I was talking to you. I overheard the conversation you had with her and can let you know we are involved with Michard Estates, and specifically Etienne Rivard. There's been a kidnap demand. Um, you might want to do a follow up with Michelson and get your information from that source?"

"Thank you, Ted. I will, and I'll watch myself with Keleher. Appreciate the information."

"Gotta go."

The call ended as Dorothy parked her Jeep in front of Maxwell's. She needed to get her thoughts in order before contacting Xander Michelson. And contact him she would.

After checking in with the staff on duty, she advised she'd be out for a while, but would return to be on hand before the dinner crowd. A few last-minute instructions to Colleen and she left. She stood for a moment before getting into her vehicle and took in the cloudless blue sky. Any day without rain was a good one for her.

***

Dorothy pulled into the driveway of the home she now shared with her father and stepmother. So far, the arrangement was working well. Dorothy needed her space, and privacy, and the recent renovations gave each their own separate areas. The lawn was littered with a carpet of colorful leaves, and she gave an eye to the eavestrough and gutters. They'd need cleaning. Another "to-do" for her list.

After making coffee, she retreated to the office, once Paul's, but now her own. Time to do some digging. She'd involve Rolin and HB once she had a better handle on what exactly might be happening with Xander Michelson and Etienne Rivard.

She'd begin with information on Michard Estates. Much would be public knowledge and easier to find. Personal data gathering would require more effort.

She didn't regret handing over the day-to-day of Quail International to HB, because she enjoyed running Maxwell's Bar and Grill with Rolin. But there were times it still felt good to return to her roots. Gaining a respect for the law and seeking justice for those wronged had been born during her time as a patrol cop back in Boston. She'd turned her skills to private investigating after moving to the Portland area many years ago.

Out of habit, she opened the top drawer of the desk and placed a container of chocolate-covered almonds next to her notebook. Coffee and chocolate – now she was ready to start work.

CHAPTER FOUR

Dorothy stared out of the office window onto a small garden. She smiled at a small section dedicated to herbs. Her dad loved to cook. So, for him, and Alanna, to have a ready supply of basil, chives and other varieties meant no shortage of mouth-watering meals she often enjoyed with them. A path from the garden meandered down to the slow-moving Willamette River. The trees lining the riverbank were shedding their leaves, which were being tossed around by a soft breeze. The house she'd shared with Paul was only a short distance away from the Marina where the *Aye?* — office of Quail International — was moored and near Maxwell's.

Coming out of her reverie, she began her search for information to better understand this strange case she'd been drawn into. People, and what made them tick, always intrigued her. As with any new case to investigate, Dorothy loved a clean slate and building a profile of those involved. She opened a new file on her computer and began with the basics of Michard Estates Winery and its owners, past and present.

The business partnership between Rivard and Michelson went back twenty-five years but was now kaput. Presumably they had, at one time, been good friends. Especially considering Etienne's daughter, Charlotte, was Xander's goddaughter.

The file grew with additions of online information. She'd need to verify salient points, but she began to develop a framework around Etienne the winemaker and Xander the administrator who was also in charge of marketing. She sipped her coffee. So where had it all gone wrong? The partnership had been in place for a long time. She made a note to speak with the employees knowing there is always one who likes to gossip — specifically when she came across the news of a nasty divorce between Rivard and his wife, Olivia St John-Rivard. She realized she had a possible case to work on, and it would mean involving others on her team. She'd have HB make enquiries about Kevin 'Frisco' Butler.

She'd also need to talk to her dad. If he'd heard any rumors about the winery when he'd been behind the bar and in charge.

The list of unanswered questions grew. She drafted up an email for Rolin and HB to see if they were around for a meeting later this evening, and attached a copy of her preliminary findings for them to discuss. She leaned back in her chair and stretched her arms over her head, then amended the email. What she needed to discuss was whether they thought this was a case to take on. She hadn't confirmed this with Xander Michelson. Everything she'd done so far was prep work and could come to nothing. Still, it was better to be prepared. Then, and only then, would this non-case become active. Especially as there was nothing official from the police or Xander himself at this point. She could hear her dad telling her not to put the cart before the horse. Still, a kidnap demand made this serious business.

Dorothy felt the need for fresh air. She did some of her best thinking outside. She threw on a jacket and wandered down to the water's edge. Sitting on the bench positioned under a tree she pondered on the questions she'd drawn up. Xander Michelson was top of her list, and she took out her cell to arrange a meeting with him - the sooner the better. She left a message and hoped he would respond.

And why was Shelby Keleher so hostile toward her? She sat musing on Keleher's reaction toward her when her phone rang. It was Xander. They arranged to meet.

***

Dorothy checked in with staff at Maxwell's as it was near dinner time and she didn't think she'd be there as promised, but Colleen had things under control.

She met Xander at a Water Street coffee shop and was surprised to see him so casually dressed. But what struck her most was the angry man's haggard face. When he glanced up at her arrival, his eyes had a haunted look.

Had she got him all wrong? She still mistrusted him, but his distress appeared genuine. She moved into the booth opposite him and waited on him to say something. A server arrived with two coffees.

"I hope you like cappuccino. I took the liberty of ordering for you, but I can get you something else."

"It's fine. Thank you for agreeing to see me."

"Like I said before, I knew you would - so what changed your mind?"

She chose her words carefully. "Mr. Michelson, Xander, the last time we spoke you were very angry, and I dismissed your concerns for Mr. Rivard as a non-issue since nothing had happened. I've since learned your former partner may have disappeared. And Kevin Butler, you mentioned him when we talked earlier? What's the connection?"

Xander worked to control his anger. "I... I *told* you this would happen. If Frisco has disappeared ... you're the detective."

She kept her cool, not reacting to his vitriol. "Before I can take this on as a bonafide case I need a few questions answered."

"What kind of questions? I had a feeling things would escalate when I heard about Butler fighting with Etienne. I told you all that. But you wouldn't listen! Find Frisco. You'll get your answers there." He let his body slam back against the chair and crossed his arms over his chest.

She held up her hand. "Take a breath, please. My biggest question is, why would you be so concerned for the man who broke up your partnership? And from what I understand, bankrupted you. More than enough reason to bring you under suspicion yourself if anything has happened to Etienne."

He uncrossed his arms, leaned forward, and blurted out his biggest concern was for Charlotte. "She's my goddaughter and at a very vulnerable age. If anything happens to her father ... I was the one who hired that cretin, Butler."

She watched him slump back against his seat, this time more exhausted than angry. She allowed him to recover for a moment. Which he soon did.

He took a controlled breath. "So, Dorothy — can I call you that? — tell me what, and how, you learned about Etienne's disappearance."

This was better, she was back in control. "Michard Estates is one of our suppliers and the driver mentioned Etienne's disappeared without a trace. What can you add?"

He leaned forward. "It was yesterday. Charlotte's 14th birthday. I'd been invited to celebrate. Etienne hadn't shown up, but business issues often take priority over family. We weren't too concerned. Until ..."

"Until what, exactly?" Dorothy wanted him to reveal the ransom demand.

Xander leaned in closer across the table and lowered his voice. "It came to the door."

"What did?"

"The note. Charlotte opened it and gave it to me."

"A note?"

"For ransom."

Finally, now it was out in the open. "Etienne's been kidnapped?"

His head sank into his hands, and he mumbled. "Yes."

Out came her notebook. "Right. What did the note say?"

"$450,000. Typed. No police and further instructions to come."

"But you've gone to the police I assume?"

He glared at her. "You weren't going to help, so I had to!"

She put up a hand to calm him down while she thought. She couldn't connect the dots. If the police were involved, this would have nothing to do with her now. "So, there's nothing more for me to do. You have your satisfaction telling me you were right all along. The police will be in charge. I can't get involved."

"No wait. I still need your help."

"With what? I don't see how I can be involved in this at all."

"Listen. Past history. Etienne and I had bad blood when the partnership broke up. I, well, you'll hear about it. I had an affair with his wife. I might not be proud of it now — seeing as she ditched me. But the police will see me as a suspect, don't you see?"

This could be interesting. What's his game? Her radar ramped up. For now, she'd see where this might play out. But she couldn't directly interfere with the police either. Well, if nothing else, she loved a challenge.

"Oh, no doubt you will be a suspect - big time. But depending on what you tell me now will determine whether I can be of any help. You need to be honest with me and answer all my questions. Got it?"

"Understood. Listen, it's not just me I'm concerned about. Charlotte has no other family. I've no idea where her mother is, and if Etienne doesn't turn up, I'm all she has. Do you see? Do you understand? The police won't care if she goes into foster care." He pushed both hands through his hair and spoke, as if to himself. "Maybe it's a good thing I'm here after all. Someone needs to keep the winery going."

"So, you've stepped back into your old role?"

"What?" He appeared startled, unaware he'd spoken aloud. "Right. Well, worst case scenario. If Etienne ... The winery is Charlotte's financial future, and I have a responsibility toward her."

Dorothy considered, while fighting her annoyance at his habit of unfinished sentences. His worry over Charlotte came across as legitimate, but something didn't ring true. For that reason alone, she'd carry on.

"I need to know everything. The affair, the business problems, and where is Charlotte's mother?"

"Since I've been out of the picture for some time, on all levels, I'm not sure where Olivia is. She hasn't even been in touch with her own daughter! The rest I will tell you as much as I can."

Dorothy's pen raced across the pages as Xander talked, about their business history, their friendship, the affair and anything else he could think of. His voice rose and fell with emotions ranging from anger to despair.

"And Olivia dumped you, then, after you were no longer, um, a financial catch?"

"Pretty much, yes. The bitch."

Ouch, but probably accurate. Dorothy now pictured a shallow, self-centered, gold-digger.

She finally laid her pen down, her thoughts swirling. "This gives me a lot to go on. I'd strongly suggest you always make yourself accessible to the police. Be upfront with them and be there for Charlotte. My team and I will see about finding Ms. St John-Rivard, and what other information we can uncover that will put you in a better light." And then she had to ask.

"And Xander? You're not involved with the kidnapping - truth?"

He sputtered and his face grew red. "I thought you were on my side. Has this been a colossal waste of time?"

"Answer the question, please."

"Of course, I'm not involved. Satisfied?"

"It had to be asked. The police will do the same. Now go home. I need to discuss this with my team, and I'll be in touch. Can I always reach you at this same number? Is there a home phone?"

He scribbled a number. "Etienne's landline at the house. I'm staying there with Charlotte."

"Fine, thank you." She closed her notebook and stood. "Call me if anything changes. Oh, and I'll send you my billing structure." That led to another question. "Tell me how you've been making a living these past few years?"

He fidgeted for a moment. "Once an entrepreneur, you know. A few side lines, enough to pay the bills. And a fall back on my savings."

Sidelines or shady dealings? Something else for her to check.

She drained her cappuccino, stood and took her leave. Time to turn her mind back to the dinner crowd at Maxwell's.

CHAPTER FIVE

Rolin, along with HB, had listened to Dorothy's retelling of her afternoon meeting with Xander Michelson. The three friends held their meeting in Rolin's office. "I can see why you want to take this on, Dee, but I should caution you this might not go over well with the police if they feel you are interfering with an active investigation."

"I understand, Rolin, and your advice is appreciated. But until I'm told to back off from this, well, you know me. I'll reconsider my options at that point. For now, I don't see you need to be involved. Other than ..."

"Checking into the legal history of the partnership between Michelson and Rivard, correct?"

"Correct. In particular regarding the loophole that Xander seems to think Etienne may have built into it right from the beginning. It's what he feels Etienne used to dissolve the partnership. I'd like to think it's a loophole that would have been beneficial to either of them, but you are the legal expert."

She turned to her right-hand man. "What's on your mind, HB?"

"I can't help thinking the name Xander Michelson is familiar." He stood. "Let me take a break for a minute. It'll come to me." He left, closing Rolin's exterior office door behind him, leaving in its wake a faint scent of burning leaves.

Rolin understood HB better now — after their time in Detroit — how he disliked staying still and would think best on his feet. The night was clear and not cold, so he assumed

HB would pace along the marina waterfront until the elusive information revealed itself to him. He focused on Dorothy. Thinking about Detroit refreshed memories of how close he'd come to losing both her and HB. The thought was pushed aside, and he came back to the present.

"HB's not the only one who thinks names are familiar. I'll have to check, Dee, but I believe I might know the St John family. Not an uncommon name, but worth a look."

Rolin recognized HB did a lot of the leg work for many of their cases, so he was pleased he might be able to contribute information as well. He felt he should caution Dorothy about the police. "You know, it's only a matter of time before your new best friend, Keleher, finds out you're working this case from another angle. Maybe you should be upfront with her."

Dorothy closed her notebook. "You're probably right, but for now I'd prefer not to deal with her. If she's as protocol driven as I think, she'll never give Xander a chance to prove he's not involved. I mean, really, if I were her, I'd be questioning him."

Rolin didn't disagree. He wouldn't be surprised if Keleher were more like Dorothy than she'd like to admit.

"I hope HB can sniff out additional information from his friends in the police department. He'll have to be careful as well. I'd hate for that avenue to be closed to us." Meaning the subject of Keleher was closed, for now.

The door opened and HB strode back inside, a somewhat smug expression on his face. "I remembered, Boss. Michelson, or as I know him — 'Stonefist Sandy' — works out at the same boxing gym I do. *Knockdown Warriors*. He's not in my weight class, but I've seen him go a few rounds. Quick on his feet and a right hook that meant lights out for more than one opponent."

Rolin heard the excitement in Dorothy's voice. "That's brilliant, HB. You can nose around the gym and see what others think of him. Two things I can think of right off. Does anyone know how he's been earning money the past few years, and what's his temper like. I'll leave it with you to dig as much as you feel you need to."

"On it first thing tomorrow, Boss."

Rolin's cell chirped, but he let it go to voicemail. "Right. We have our assignments then. And I also have court in the morning, so unless there's anything else, maybe we should call it a night?"

He didn't miss the puzzled look on Dorothy's face, but he had a call to respond to. He'd talk to her later.

***

Dorothy said goodnight to HB and made her final check on the bar before calling it a done day herself. Driving home she tried to pinpoint the uncharacteristic brush off from Rolin. She'd thought they had more to discuss, but the phone call he'd not answered had signaled a change in the atmosphere. Or was she imagining it? Likely a client he needed to talk to in confidence. But then why didn't he just say so?

Never mind. She had notes to update and thought her dad would like to know Xander Michelson was now a client. A client who needed to be sent billing information. Maybe she'd spend some time searching online for Oliva St John-Rivard. What a mouthful. She couldn't believe a mother would abandon her child and not be in touch over the years. Why some women blew the privilege of motherhood she'd never understand. And there it was, again. Paul's death meant there'd be no chance now for her either. Even though her age was pushing it, she and Paul had discussed taking a chance to have a child. Don't go there!

She forced herself to think about Xander Michelson, and wondered how he and Charlotte were coping. Was there the off-chance Etienne had escaped? Doubtful, but she'd call Xander when she got home.

Once home, and changed into more casual clothes, she knocked on the connecting door to her father's apartment. Invited in, she was offered a nightcap by Alanna, and she recounted the twisted case of kidnapping and betrayal. Thoughts of Rolin's brusque goodnight and the loss of Paul were pushed to an upper shelf in her mind.

***

Rolin regretted ending the evening in a hurry with Dorothy and HB, but he needed to respond to the call he'd left unanswered. Hearing the voice, an unmistakable combination of sass and silk, left him no doubt who had called. "Hello, Anjali. It's been a long time."

CHAPTER SIX

HB was an early riser. The *Aye* rocked gently beneath his feet as he downed his first coffee of the day. He wouldn't brag to just anyone, but not many could brew coffee to match his own. After sending instructions to the investigators he managed, he scribbled notes on last night's meeting with Dorothy and Rolin. Methodical and totally focused he referred to his list of what he wanted to discuss with his police contact. He still held hope Etienne Rivard had been found and the case focus could shift. But, no. He'd have heard from his contacts.

A loner by choice, HB had few friends outside of the Dennehys and Rolin, except for a veteran of the Portland Police Bureau, Detective Jake Warner. Injured a year ago, while tackling a murder suspect, he'd been assigned light desk duties until cleared for active duty. HB and Jake had bonded, after a fashion, during the investigation into the murder of Dorothy's fiancé, Paul Webster. Their friendship was mutually beneficial, centered around cases HB worked, in which Jake would pass on relevant information. And vice versa as HB often gave him a heads up on street activity. They shared a similar work ethic and thought alike - two peas in a pod.

While HB planned his day, his ear was tuned into his police scanner and he heard about the usual B and Es, and fender benders reported in the city during the morning rush hour, but nothing about a disappearance or kidnap.

Checking online also left him empty handed. The kidnap hadn't been announced in either the *Oregonian* or on social media sites. HB had questions. No doubt the ransom note insisted on no police contact or any publicity. He doubted the silence would last long. Invariably, news of a kidnap broke at some point. The police would lose the upper hand once that happened.

HB took out his phone. "Jake. It's HB. How's the leg?"

The raspy long-time smoker's voice responded with a growl. "Slow going, man. What's up?"

"Wondered if you can get away for a break. I need your input. Today if possible."

Jake snorted. "Let me guess. You have questions about something you think I have the answers for. I thought I might be hearing from you. Noon - Starbucks on 2nd street. The pumpkin latte will be on you."

The call disconnected, which suited HB. Irrelevant pleasantries irked him and often made him uncomfortable. Sitting in the operations room of Quail Investigations he contemplated his life aboard the *Aye*. This job and his living quarters were perfect for a man married to his occupation. He rolled his shoulders - he'd been sitting too long. He added to his questions for Jake and then made a note to drop by Knockdown Warriors after seeing the cop. He'd see what others thought of Stonefist Sandy. He sent a quick email to Dorothy, advising her of his day's plan.

***

Arriving at Starbucks ten minutes late he spied Jake in a booth sipping on his latte – a half-eaten turkey wrap in front of him. Starbucks was not to HB's liking. Too yuppie for him. He ordered a black coffee and slid into the bench opposite the detective.

"Sorry I'm late. Thanks for seeing me. I'm looking for answers on a case, and you're my best bet."

Jake took another swallow of his pumpkin latte. "No worries. You made it sound urgent."

HB laid it out based on what he'd learned from Dorothy, then sat back, while Jake attacked the remainder of his lunch wrap with nicotine-stained fingers. Neither man was a gregarious talker and HB knew not to interrupt his lunch companion. Jake would be mulling over the information while he chewed. They both understood the value of listening and observing before saying much.

When Jake's plate was empty, he used a napkin to clean up crumbs, and then pointed to his empty coffee mug. HB went to the counter and ordered another coffee for Jake.

"Not having another? Or is payday too far off?"

HB grouched. "I'll be wired if I have any more coffee today. So, tell me. Have you heard anything about this case? So far, there's nothing online, social media or the local papers."

Jake deflected the question. "No doubt you've heard we've a new — temporary — Sergeant in the department. A real ball breaker. Shelby Keleher. Strictly by the book. I'll have to train her my way if she's here long enough."

"Yes, Dorothy wasn't impressed. Got the impression she has no time for P.I.s."

"Drop by and meet her yourself, man. Turn on the charm you keep hidden."

HB snorted, "Yeah right. That's me. Casanova! Later maybe. Back to what she knows."

"Right. Well, Keleher appears to be keeping this one under wraps. The note said not to contact the police, as usual. So, the activity has to be lowkey and not jeopardize the victim. The usual process of who and why. Xander Michelson's name came up as a person of interest."

"He's next on my list after I leave here. As luck would have it, we box at the same gym. Knockdown Warriors. If I turn up anything useful, maybe I'll introduce myself to Keleher. But Dorothy's first — she's the one who pays me. Not the cops."

Jakes' phone chirped. "Got to take this. Don't go yet."

HB nodded, and watched his friend's face scowl as he took the call and responded curtly. "I'll be there in five." Jake stared at HB. "What was the name again of the guy Rivard had a fight with?"

"Kevin Butler, aka Frisco."

"Game on, then. Shit's going to hit the fan now. He's been found. Dead. At the winery. You didn't hear it from me — got it? I have to get back to the station. My light duties include press liaison, so Keleher needs me. Goes without saying, anything you can share with me I'll do the same."

They stood, and HB slapped Jake on the shoulder. "I'll be in touch."

Jake moved ahead of HB; his limp still noticeable. They hit the street, moving in opposite directions, but Jake gave HB a thumbs up before he turned toward his unmarked patrol car.

Kidnap, and now a murder. What would he learn at Knockdown Warriors? Something seemed off about this Xander Michelson and the gym might reveal grounds for his concern. But first he needed to make a call. "Boss, we have a body."

CHAPTER SEVEN

"The plot thickens, HB. And Jake will keep you updated?"

"As much as he can, Boss. He's got to watch his back as well. This new detective Keleher is not exactly making friends wherever she goes."

Dorothy smirked. "I don't disagree. I bet the winery will be crawling with cops. Think I'll play dumb and head out there to visit Xander."

"And I'm off to the gym to nose around. Maybe spar a round or two just to make it look good."

"Get back to me later – or sooner if it's important."

***

An hour later, Dorothy found herself at Michard Estates Winery. No surprise, a patrol car sat across the road from the entrance to a long, gravel drive. The late afternoon sun lent a golden glow to the rows and rows of grapevines on either side of the driveway. In the distance, up and down the rows, she could see large white pails standing like abandoned sentries, but no workers. She didn't know a lot about wine making, but she enjoyed the end result. The vines appeared to be healthy and weighed down with fruit. The workers would be busy with a bumper harvest – but likely all work had come to a stop with the discovery of an employee's body.

She wasn't sure she'd be allowed access, but nothing ventured, nothing gained. She turned up the driveway and could see more police presence and a white van belonging to the State Medical Examiner. The body would still be on site and Dorothy's interest grew. If cops had been standing around for a while, some might be bored and talkative. With luck, she might see a familiar face.

She pulled her Jeep off to the shoulder, her progress halted by the yellow crime scene tape. Before she could open her door, a uniformed officer tapped on her window, and motioned her to roll it down.

"I'm sorry. This is a crime scene, no access."

Dorothy didn't recognize the serious face of the young female cadet. Maybe she could bluff her way in. "Xander Michelson is expecting me." She held up her cell. "I'll call him?"

The cop nodded. Now Dorothy could only hope Xander was on the premises and would validate her presence. "Hi, Xander. Dorothy Dennehy, I'm here to see you, but the police won't let me pass. Right, one sec."

She put the phone on speaker and held it close to the open window. "This is Xander Michelson. I'm in the house and need to speak with Ms. Dennehy. Please allow her to come through. Thank you."

Moments later she pulled up near the front door of the Rivard home. It must have been part of the original homestead but had been enlarged over the years. A newer annex housed the business side of the winery. A couple of smaller, cottage size, homes were set farther back. The buildings were all coordinated with similar brick and stucco exteriors. Reddish clay roofs evoked a Spanish, or Mediterranean feel. She wondered if one of those smaller homes had been Xander's at one time. When things were better between him and Etienne Rivard.

A familiar officer stood at the front door. Perfect. "Hiya, Ted. What's going on?"

His eyes darted to the right and left. "Not surprised to see you here but be warned. She's around and probably will not be happy to see you. If you're talking with Michelson, I suggest you make it fast."

"Where is the good sergeant?"

Ted pointed off in the distance. "Behind the offices, where they keep the wine barrels. She's still with the body." He leaned behind him and opened the door. "Like I said, be warned."

"I am, and thanks."

The door closed behind her, and her eyes adjusted to the dim interior as she moved forward a few steps and called out. "Xander?"

"Who are you?" Dorothy turned to see a young girl — a teenager. Must be Charlotte. Her long dark hair had been braided with extensions of purple. A form-fitting tank top ended just above her navel, where a large silver stud jutted. Dorothy hadn't much experience with angst-driven teens and had no way of knowing whether the sullen, contemptuous look directed at her was genuine, or a reflection of fear for her father's safety.

"I'm Dorothy Dennehy, here to see Xander Michelson. Your godfather, correct? You must be Charlotte."

"What's it to you?"

Before Dorothy could formulate a suitable response, Xander came down the hallway. "Dorothy, I'm glad you're here. I see you've met Charlotte. She's very upset about her dad."

"Somebody better find him, or else." Charlotte shot a venomous look at both of them, turned and stomped off down the hallway. Seconds later a door slammed shut.

Dorothy waited on Xander to comment. His shirt was rumpled, and he hadn't shaved. "Sorry about that. She's the one who got the ransom note, so ... You've heard about Kevin Butler?"

Dorothy played her cards tight to her chest. "Only that a body has been discovered. I'm not the police, remember. So, I don't have the details. I assume there's no news on Mr. Rivard. Have the police talked with you yet?"

"Nothing! And yes, I've spoken with them briefly. It can't be a coincidence about Butler, can it?" Xander's eyes beseeched her to provide a response to make this all go away.

"Not for me to say. Listen, I can't hang around – cops don't much care for outsiders to be involved. But you can always reach me. Sometimes I, or my team, have ways of finding information the police would have a hard time getting." Xander didn't need to know HB was at the gym doing background checks.

"Good to know, thanks. I'm really concerned for Charlotte. Wish we could find her mother. Have you had any luck?"

"No, not yet, but we haven't given up. You say Charlotte got the ransom note? Tell me about it."

Xander sighed and pointed into a living area behind them. Remnants of a birthday party told the tale of a celebration abandoned. Unused paper plates, and wrapped presents mocked the atmosphere hanging over the home. "We'd planned a great party, but then Etienne disappeared. Charlotte called her friends to cancel, and everything went on hold. Then the doorbell rang, and Charlotte went to answer. She thought it was a friend who hadn't heard the party was off. But no, a courier with a package for her. She signed for it and came back here. She thought it was another birthday gift — not likely from her mother though." He sighed. "As if. Anyway, she opened it, and it was the ransom note. At first, we thought it was a joke, but the package contained a silver neck chain. Etienne's. Charlotte recognized it at once because she'd given it to him on his last birthday."

So, the kidnapper obviously knew enough about Etienne to send the necklace and note directly to Charlotte. Cruel, but effective. And narrowed the list of suspects, which Dorothy was sure the police already knew.

Through a window, she saw the coroner's vehicle driving away. No doubt Kevin Butler's body inside and off to the morgue for an autopsy. A call to Lucas might yield useful information. No need to share the fact she had a family contact in the coroner's office with Xander.

Xander sank into a chair behind him, as deflated as the party balloons nearby. He ran his hands through his wavy black hair. "What will happen if Etienne ..."

Dorothy didn't let him finish. "The police are good at their jobs. I know they will do everything in their power to find him."

"We most certainly will. Who let you in here?"

Dorothy whirled to find Shelby Keleher striding through the doorway. Her face was grim and her eyes lasered into Dorothy.

"Sergeant. Nice to see you again, except for the circumstances. Xander has engaged my services so I'm here to consult with him."

"I would say your services are no longer needed. This is a crime scene, and you need to leave." She hesitated. "Will I be able to reach you, if need be?"

"Of course. Anything I can do to help."

Keleher inspected the business card Dorothy had handed over. "Don't be so sure it's your help we need. Right now, you're a person of interest in the death of Kevin Butler."

Dorothy bristled but didn't rise to the bait. Keleher was going by the book and Dorothy had her own book of rules. "I understand, but I'm sure you'll soon see I've no connection to Kevin Butler and this is the first time I've ever been here. Of course, I'll answer any questions to help."

Dorothy couldn't read Keleher's reaction. The sergeant had perfected a stone-face, as she looked from Dorothy to Michelson. "Exactly what is the nature of your business here?"

Before Dorothy could explain, Xander jumped in. "My fault, Sergeant. Ms. Dennehy isn't involved with finding Etienne. I had asked her to try and find Olivia, Charlotte's mother. No one seems to know where she is. She needs to be here with her daughter, don't you see?"

"I see alright." Keleher focused on Dorothy. "We need to talk. Be in my office later today. But for now, you're done here. Understood?"

Dorothy knew not to push her luck and told Xander she'd be in touch with any information on Olivia as soon as possible.

She turned to leave, nearly colliding with a uniform who rushed in. "Sarge. We've located the victim's car. Abandoned."

Keleher had her phone to her ear before the officer finished speaking, and barked orders. "Get forensics. Rivard's car has been found. Move!"

CHAPTER EIGHT

HB pulled open the front door to his favorite gym. Although the aroma of sweat mingling with stale air was probably the same in other places, HB found himself most comfortable at Knockdown Warriors. Nothing fancy, no saunas or juice bar, just punching bags, a couple of rings and showers. He'd been coming here for more years than he could remember, and Amos Agnew, the proprietor, ran a clean establishment. HB made sure of that. Frequent background checks ensured all was above board. Couldn't say the same about some of the other gyms in town.

A great place to work out frustrations and no need to make small talk. He knew some of the members by name, but HB preferred to keep his private life private. His one concession was to allow Amos the privilege of calling him Holden. Not too many would dare.

Amos, with his sweat stained shirt, and towel hanging around his neck, greeted HB. "Holden, my man. It's been a couple of weeks. You need to do some venting?"

"Something like that. Anyone available to go a couple of rounds?"

Amos scanned the gym. It was fairly quiet at the moment but wouldn't be long before the place began jumping with keen boxers and stay-fit fanatics stopping in to burn off the day before heading home.

The owner yelled across the space. "Milos – you were looking for a partner. Holden here, the same."

He punched HB in the shoulder. "My matchmaking is done. Have at it."

HB greeted Milos. He was of average build, maybe an inch taller than HB's 5'4" frame, but in really good shape and possibly five years younger. Tight abs glistened. HB pegged him as a serious contender, and he'd likely have to work hard to keep up. He grunted a greeting to his new partner. "Give me a minute to change. Be right back."

Ten minutes later, HB struggled to match Milos's intensity. And because he was at the gym for more than exercise, he needed to call it quits while he could. He let Milos get a punch in and the ref called it.

Milos bounced back and forth on his feet. He might be up for more, but HB was done. "You're too good for me, pal. But thanks for the workout."

Milos spat out his mouth guard into his gloved hand. "You've done a few rounds in your time. Nice right hook you've got there."

They jumped from the ring and walked toward the locker room.

HB had his opening. "Well, my right hook is nothing compared to Stonefist Sandy. Not in my class though."

"Yeah, me either. Too tall. But he can fight. Bet he could have been a pro in his younger years."

"You know him at all? I've been coming here for years and only seen him a few times. Heard he owns a winery. Have to keep in shape for all the cork pulling I guess."

They shared a laugh and sat on a bench in front of a bank of lockers.

Milos didn't need prompting, so HB let him tell all. "The winery. Right. Fact is, he only used to own a winery. Got on the outs with his partner a few years back. Must have pissed him off some – and I think he took it out on whoever he boxed with."

"Did he ever say what happened?" HB feigned interest in peeling the Velcro back on his gloves but was all ears.

"Not so much. I gather woman trouble. Bit of an arrogant prick, come to think of it. The way he talked about her and the winery. Like the whole world was against him. You know the type?"

HB nodded. "Only too well, my friend. Wonder if he'll show up here today – does he come here regularly?"

Milos furrowed his brow. "Come to think of it, he's here two, three times a week, but can't remember the last time I saw him. Amos would know. And now I'm curious. He's always going on about some new business or other, looking for investors. Must make some money at whatever he does. I avoid him when he starts talking about quick returns. If it sounds too good to be true ..."

"... it probably is. I hear ya. I'd avoid it as well." HB stood. "Thanks for the workout, Milos. It's shower time now and then I'm outta here. I'll go rounds with you again, for sure. You'll keep me on my toes."

"Likewise. Holden, right?"

HB snorted. "Pal, you can call me HB."

***

Dorothy's text had HB driving in the direction of her home. She'd added that Max insisted he come with a hearty appetite for dinner. He smiled to himself as he drove - say no to a meal prepared by Max? Never. Microwaved dinners aboard the *Aye* had long lost their appeal.

He parked on the street, leaving the driveway free for Dorothy. She wasn't home yet, so HB went round the side of the house to knock on the door of Max and Alanna's new address.

Max swung the door wide. "Come on in, son. There's a chill in the air tonight - can I get you a wee nip of something before dinner?"

"Er, no thanks, unless you have my favorite brew?" He thrust a bottle-shaped bag into Max's beefy hands. "Here, I got you and Alanna a housewarming gift I think you'll like." Buying gifts was right up there with small talk in HB's book - he never knew what was appropriate. "I would have bought the single malt, but Dorothy doesn't pay me enough."

Max burst out laughing and ushered him in. "Ah. Good choice, my son. Jameson. Just what the doctor ordered." Before HB could answer, Alanna joined them.

"So, what did the doctor order?" HB, always comfortable with Max and their long history, still felt out of place with Alanna. She could be intimidating, although she'd never directed it at him.

Her face flashed a smile "Oh, a lovely bottle of Jameson. Thank you, HB." She took the bottle from Max and poked him in the chest with it. "Your doctor told you to lay off the drink so all the more for me. It will go fine with the soda bread I've just made." She whirled away, leaving HB doubting the wisdom of his purchase. And not entirely sure she wasn't upset with his gift. Alanna went back to the kitchen, and they could hear her humming. HB took that as a good sign she wasn't upset - too much.

She shouted back to them. "Dorothy and Rolin will be here any minute so make yourselves comfy." Then she poked her head round the corner and pointed her wooden spoon in his direction. "I'm counting on you to keep an eye on him, HB."

HB mumbled, "Yes ma'am," and tried to keep a straight face as he watched the frustration build in Max.

Max tried to come across as upset, but HB knew he doted on Alanna, and generally forgave her efforts to monitor his health. "That woman would drive me to drink - if it was allowed. You can't have this, you can't have that." His bark was worse than his bite, but HB figured he was feeling the restrictions a little more than usual.

HB, who stayed single after his fiancé's tragic death years ago, tried to placate his good friend. "She means well Max, for your own good."

"Yes, well, I get plenty of flak from Dorothy. So enough about me. What's happening with this latest case?"

"I'd prefer to wait until the boss is here and then I won't be repeating anything. You understand. I haven't got the latest from her either."

"That'll be them now," said Max as the door opened after a brief knock. Dorothy, with a smile for her dad, entered ahead of Rolin, who held a bouquet of flowers for Alanna.

She gave her father a hug. "What is that heavenly aroma? Have you been baking, Dad?"

Max kissed his girl, shook hands with Rolin and accepted the flowers from him. "Some of your favorite soda bread, my

girl. Tonight, though, we'll see how Alanna's bread measures up
- I've been giving her some pointers on Irish cooking, don't you
know. But seems like it's to be flowers for me instead of a bottle
of Jameson's finest." Max nodded his head in HB's direction. "A
very thoughtful gift from your number one, darlin', but my wife
has commandeered it."

Alanna came from the kitchen wiping her hands on her
apron. She greeted her guests, then looked over at her husband.
"Don't blame me, it's his doctor who told him to cut back on
drinking with his heart condition. I'm just enforcing it." She
planted a kiss on Max's cheek. "But he can still pour you one.
Would you do the honors, darling?"

***

"My compliments to both of you," said Rolin, patting his
stomach. "One of these days I might try my hand at Haitian
Griyo — one of my favored childhood dishes — to share with
you."

"Which is, what exactly?" teased Dorothy

"Baked pork shoulder. And perhaps accompanied by Pen
Patat - a sweet potato pudding."

"Bring it on," said HB, who managed to stifle a small burp.
"Ah, sorry. But it does mean I enjoyed my meal."

The table shared a laugh at HB's expense, but it made him
feel good to be included. These four were the closest he had to
family.

"Rolin's right, Dad. Your stew was delicious as always. And
Alanna? Your bread will give him a run for his money." She laid
her napkin across her empty plate. "So now, I'm guessing it's

time to get down to business. HB and I gathered information today and didn't come up empty-handed."

Alanna stood. "Before you start, let me dish out dessert."

Over delicious apple cake — in HB's opinion — Dorothy recounted her visit to the winery and her encounter with the charming Shelby Keleher. HB then added his take on Xander Michelson.

"I don't know, Boss. Something about that guy." He was pleased when Dorothy nodded.

"Me too. It might be the stress he's under and worry over Charlotte, but he bears keeping a close eye on."

Her phone, sitting in her handbag across the room, buzzed. "I'd better get that." She retrieved it, read the screen, and looked at the group.

"Text from Ted, on the qt of course. Who wants to guess what was found on Kevin Butler's body?"

HB expectantly waited, along with the others. "Tell us, Boss."

"A *copy* of the ransom note."

CHAPTER NINE

Dorothy needed no excuse to bring the evening to an end with her father and Alanna. Her dad understood her compulsion to get to work - especially when she had an interesting case. So, after helping with the cleanup, she, Rolin and HB moved into her part of the house to discuss what had been learned.

"Perfect timing," commented Rolin as they made themselves comfortable. He looked at his phone. "I was waiting for confirmation on a legal aspect of the partnership agreement Rivard and Michelson had. I, uh, have a contact who specializes in corporate law. Her name is Anjali Varma, and she was able to clarify some points for me, that is, us."

Dorothy found it interesting Rolin appeared uncomfortable mentioning his contact's name. The same way he'd acted when he'd dismissed talking with her the other night, after his phone rang. She was curious but it would have to wait.

"But first, Boss, tell us more about this ransom note. What about the one already delivered to the family?"

"Not much else to go on for now, HB. Ted only knows the note has been taken for comparison against the first. On the surface, they appear identical. Something I've never come across – two versions of a ransom note?"

"Is there anything confirmed about the cause of death for Kevin Butler?" asked Rolin.

"Again, information is bare bones I'm afraid. Initial reports show he slipped on wine leaking from a barrel, and fell backwards, hitting his head on the concrete floor. We'll have to wait for the autopsy results to learn more. I have a call in to Lucas who's agreed to let me know if anything interesting turns up during the autopsy."

"Haven't seen your cousin in a while, Dee. Is he still working his way up the ladder over at the coroner's office?" asked Rolin.

"He mentioned a couple of upcoming retirements, so he plans to apply for a more senior role, yes."

"So, what's next, Boss?"

Dorothy eyed her trusted colleague. "Since you've asked so nicely, I'd like you to be the sole contact with the police, for as long as possible. You know Jake Warner, in addition to my contact, Ted Jellico. Your choice who to talk with but keep me posted. For now, I'd prefer to keep a safe distance from Keleher, but we need to have inside information and Ted is our best bet on that score. See what you can arrange in the morning?"

"I'm on it. I have a feeling you two need to talk on the legal angle of things. I'll leave you to it, okay?" He sprang to his feet, not waiting for an answer.

Dorothy nodded and rose to her feet. "Off you go. We'll touch base tomorrow."

HB shoved his ball cap back on his head as he moved to the front door. "'Nite Boss. Rolin." And he was gone.

Dorothy shook her head as she closed the door behind him. "He just can't sit still, can he?" But her tone understanding. She knew HB never liked to stay put in one place for long.

"Aside from that, HB's worth his weight in gold, which I'm sure you're aware of. Now, ready to talk legal?"

"Can you stand more coffee before we start?"

"Good idea. And you might want your notebook to take down a few critical points I have for you."

"Give me five minutes and I'll be back with both."

When she returned, she found Rolin had moved from the sofa and now stood in front of a photo display she'd arranged on a side table. She put the tray of coffee down and joined him. The framed pictures were of various groupings, but each one showed Paul. With Rolin, with HB, Max and Alanna, and more than one of just Paul and herself. Moments captured of a special time in her life.

They didn't speak, silently sharing memories. Finally, Dorothy laid her hand on Rolin's arm and simply said, "I know."

Rolin smiled at her. "Yes."

They sat side by side on the sofa and sipped their coffee. "We haven't done this for a while, have we?" asked Dorothy. "I'm glad you're able to help out on this case. But we still have a bar to look after."

"Which is why we have staff. But you're right, and I have a practice to maintain as well. We'll manage."

"Right," said Dorothy as she opened her notebook. "What have you got?"

"A little background first. For what it's worth, I do know the St John family, although I've never met Olivia St John-Rivard. Years ago, her father was dealing with a potential embezzler, and he needed advice, which I provided. On a side note, the pandemic did a financial number on the family. Most of their wealth is based on clothing design and manufacture — the fashion district in New York, you know? So, the kidnapper better not be counting on any piles of money from that side of the family. I also did a little digging into Etienne Rivard. Because he's the current sole owner of the winery there's more information available on him. Apparently, he's well known for his high moral standards, a result of his upbringing as far as I can tell. Anyway, you'll see how this plays out in respect to the business partnership."

"I somehow don't see Xander Michelson sharing the same standards."

"Go it in one, Dee. Which is why Rivard had a morals clause written into the partnership agreement. It focused on two areas. One, social — as in social media — standards, and two, individual, personal standards."

"Unusual in a business partnership, but Etienne must have had concerns about his friend. Smart move on his part, I'd say." And then she had it. "The affair and the divorce — that's how he used the loophole!"

"Revenge on his part, perhaps. But there's more."

"And?"

"To get the business off the ground required substantial capital. Etienne had an inheritance which more than covered his share, but Xander struggled to match it. I need to dig more, but I believe he had to beg, borrow, and steal from various sources. Including Etienne."

Dorothy laid her pen down and flexed her fingers. "This is terrific, Rolin. You'll have to pass on my thanks to your friend – Anjali? – as well."

"Well, you might be able to do that yourself, in person. Ann is in town for a while. She lives in London, but is in Portland on business, in addition to helping me with understanding this loophole. We've known each other a long time."

The suggestion provoked an unfamiliar feeling in her, as if her ribs were being squeezed. "Yes, of course, sounds like a good idea. Whenever you like." She needed to end this line of questions and part of her hoped the meeting would never come about. Why?

The smile on Rolin's face made her think he'd been anxious about asking her to meet his friend. Again, why?

Let it go, girl.

"You've given me a lot of food for thought." She closed her notebook. "Do you want any more coffee, or should we call it a night?"

Rolin checked his watch. "It's later than I thought, so I'd better be on my way. Sleep well, Dee."

She walked him to the door and stood watching as he drove away.

Yes, she had a lot to think about, and not all of it involved the case.

CHAPTER TEN

HB settled for the evening in his living quarters aboard the *Aye*. He mulled over what he'd learned about the disappearance — no, it was officially a kidnapping — of the vineyard owner. Some things were not sitting well with him, especially Xander Michelson. And now the death of the one person of interest Michelson had mentioned during his first meeting with Dorothy. Frisco Butler.

HB rarely needed to refer to notes due to his photographic memory. A talent not everyone was aware of, other than Dorothy. But, now that he was in charge, he needed to keep actual records of all clients and cases taken on. Mumbling to himself he recorded all he'd heard tonight and what he'd learned about Xander at the gym. Before turning in for the night he texted Jake asking for a short meeting in the morning. If he didn't hear back, he'd show up anyway and hoped to eye the dragon lady they kept talking about.

He went to sleep puzzling over Xander Michelson.

***

HB followed the desk duty escort to Keleher's department, although he was familiar with its location. The officer, who was another new face on the team, pointed. "Jake Warner's over there."

Jake was bent over, rifling through a desk drawer and was unaware of HB's approach.

"What you looking for in there - the way out?"

"Huh?" Jake looked up. "Oh, it's you." He shoved the desk drawer closed. "We've gotta stop meeting this way."

HB chuckled. "More like you've been privileged to have my presence twice in one week already."

HB perused the homicide department and shuddered at the desk bound officers. He'd never be chained to a desk now. The room buzzed with their voices as they answered phones and consulted with colleagues or stared at computer screens. He managed a quick glance at their incident whiteboard. Car found was circled in red. Photos of Rivard, his family, and Michelson were lined up in a neat row.

Jake lowered his voice and looked over HB's shoulder. HB followed his glance toward a glass paneled office. He couldn't resist a barb. "Pierson looks a little different these days."

"Hell, man. I wish he'd get back here. That one... Not my idea of a sarge." He turned back to HB "She's put the screws to all of us right now. Might be better we talk when her radar's not focused this way, but I don't know if she'll be leaving anytime soon. Sorry."

"Don't sweat it. I was hoping we could talk this morning, but," HB rose to his feet.

Jake groaned. "Too late. Hold onto your hat and anything else that's precious to you, if you get my drift."

HB looked over his shoulder then fully turned to take in the woman heading their way. So, this was Sergeant Keleher. Mid-thirties maybe. A couple of inches taller than him. Her uniform was spotless, her blonde hair tightly pulled back. He wondered if her face would crack under a smile. A tablet and stylus seemed part of her dress code. Everything about her said she was all business, including her refusal to acknowledge HB's presence.

"Warner. Do you have those bank statements for me on the winery?"

Jake shuffled files on his desk and handed her a sheaf of papers. "Yes, Sarge. I was just about to bring them to you ..."

"When you had an unexpected visitor. I see. Someone connected to the case I assume?"

HB was amused to see Jake's discomfort. He now better understood Dorothy's take on her. "Not exactly. This is a good friend, HB. I mean, Holden Bartholomew. He's the lead investigator ..."

"For Dorothy Dennehy's outfit. I see." She tightened her lips and her blue eyes bored into HB. "Did she not relay my message to all her people?"

HB clamped down on a smart-ass comment, and instead tipped his head. "Sergeant Keleher. Glad to meet you." He grew bolder. "Name sounds Irish?"

She blinked as if considering whether to respond. To HB's surprise, her military stance relaxed a couple of degrees. "Your detective skills are correct. Irish. A connection I seem to share with your boss. You go by HB, then?"

HB nodded, anxious more small talk would be expected, and disappointed when it wasn't.

"I suggest you conclude your business with my officer and be on your way. I'd hate to issue a formal warning to stay out of police affairs."

Without another word she turned and strode back to her office. When her door closed, Jake let out a breath. "See what

I mean. Tough as the brass on her jacket. HB?" He jabbed his friend's shoulder. "Cat got your tongue?"

"What? Oh, right, I mean no. Not quite what I expected."

"Word among the guys here is she's no dumb blonde and might even be considered attractive if she lightened up a bit."

"Yeah, she is." HB spoke more to himself than Jake, who wore a puzzled expression.

"HB? Back to business, okay? How about I meet you at Starbucks in an hour." His voice dropped. "I have something you'll want to see."

***

HB arrived first, grabbed coffee and found a table. While he waited on Jake, he found himself curious about Shelby Keleher and wondered why. So unlike Emily, or Dorothy. Something in her eyes maybe. He couldn't be sure if his instincts were warning him, or if it was mere curiosity. He put further musings aside as Jake slid into the booth across from him and pushed an envelope across the table.

"We'll have to be quick. From Ted Jellico for Dorothy. He said you could look, too."

Jake gulped his coffee as HB opened the envelope. He unfolded the paper which showed photocopied images and looked at his friend. "I heard. Unreal. Two ransom notes?"

"Yeah. But take a close look. They're not identical."

HB examined the copies. "Thoughts on this, Jake? Never heard of duplicate ransom notes before. I assume they've been fingerprinted. Which is the one Rivard's daughter got? And where was the other found?"

"The first one was given to the daughter. The second was found on Frisco Butler's body. See the difference?"

"I see it." HB pointed to the second note. "The amount of $200,000 has been crossed out on Butler's copy. The other note shows it as $450,000. Almost like this was a draft copy."

"Exactly. So, Sherlock, you can see why the case has ramped up. First a kidnapping, with a ransom demand, and then a body, with a similar note. If Kevin Butler is — was — the kidnapper, how the hell will Etienne Rivard be found? All of this is connected to the winery. And if your team doesn't already know, Kevin Butler is a known drug dealer in this area. Not smart, but nervy. Last we heard he started to specialize in 'K'. Damn, I'll be late. Listen, have your boss contact Ted for more, okay?"

"I see Rivards's car has been found? Any details?"

"Hell man, I need to go," sighed Warner, but he paused to reveal more. "It was found in the Mystic District. See what you guys can find out about Rivard. If he went there on a regular basis, someone might know. He'd be easy pickings. I don't envy the leg work the uniforms will be putting in over there."

HB folded the paper and tucked it into his jacket pocket. "Thanks for this, man. I'll be in touch, especially if I have anything worth sharing with you."

"Anytime, but not at the station, got it?"

"What? You don't want to ruffle the feathers of your by-the-book Sergeant?"

"Waste-of-time media liaison crap." Jake tapped his injured leg. "The sooner I'm back to my regular duties, the better, and get away from her. Text me, don't call on my desk line."

They parted company. HB shot a text to Dorothy.

Meet me at the Aye. Something to show you.
He didn't mention comparing notes on Keleher.

CHAPTER ELEVEN

The *Private, Aye?* had been home to Dorothy for a long time, so she didn't feel out of place meeting with HB there now.

She leaned back in her chair after she'd inspected the ransom note copies HB showed her. "So, the draft note was found on Butler's body. Interesting to say the least. Maybe Michelson had him pegged right from the start."

"Did Jellico have anything more to add when you spoke with him, Boss?"

"As expected, multiple fingerprints on the copy handed over to Charlotte, but only Butler's prints on the copy found on him. The paper used appears to be from the same stock. Nothing unusual, and from a laser printer. Dead end there."

"And nothing definitive from the autopsy?"

"Ted said the tox screen showed a .20 blood alcohol count. He would have been wasted. Trace amounts of cocaine as well, but alcohol is likely what led to him slipping and cracking his skull. That's what likely killed him. I'm waiting on a call back from Lucas, he said he might have something else for me."

Dorothy stood and took the few steps needed to reach the compact kitchen's counter, where coffee awaited. She held the pot in HB's direction. "Any more for you?"

"I'm good, thanks."

Before she sat back down, she peeked into the houseboat's unique feature room, next to the kitchen. Over the years, she'd spent hours in the cramped space, running her business. Updated laptops, surveillance equipment and anything else needed for her line of work, was housed there. And now it was all HB's domain. She turned back to face him. "You're happy with this setup? If there's anything you need to make it more comfortable, let me know."

"Boss, you know me. Nothing fancy means less to take care of. Except for the electronics. Only the best for Quail. Right?"

She tipped her coffee mug in his direction. Not that she needed the reassurance, but HB was a big part of her life and she depended on him. She'd spare no expense to ensure he was happy. Well, as happy as HB was ever likely to be.

"Back to business then. Where were we?"

"You were talking about what Ted learned from the autopsy," said HB. "Has the coroner made a ruling the death was accidental?"

"Not yet. He's saying suspicious, for now. In light of the apparent connection to the kidnapping. Maybe there's another person involved. A falling out among thieves?"

HB picked up his pen. "I think one or two unofficial questions to Michard Estates staff might be in order. I can start on it tomorrow."

"Good. I had hoped to have something concrete on the whereabouts of Olivia St John-Rivard, but all my leads have drawn a blank. For a socialite, she seems to have gone off the grid since the break-up of her marriage." Dorothy sighed. "I have a feeling her wealthy family has something to do with that. Easy to lay low or disappear when you have resources."

"With better options than witness protection I bet."

Dorothy smiled. The fact HB was now able to refer to a dark time in his past meant he was coming to terms with his history. She hoped.

"You're probably right on that score. I have a couple of more possible contacts to check out before I give up." She drained her coffee. "And on that note, I need to make tracks."

"Got a date or something, Boss?"

A date. As if. "Not quite. Rolin has a lawyer friend in town he wants me to meet — in about an hour."

She opened her phone when it buzzed and read an email as she walked to the door. "And, now apparently, tomorrow I have another meeting. Sergeant Keleher wants to see me, first thing in the morning."

"On a Saturday? Guess that goes with her work mindset. I forgot to tell you, Boss. I met her today. Just watch your back is all I'm saying."

"That's what I pay you for, HB."

***

A valet parked Dorothy's Jeep. She'd never been to The Royal Sonesta, where Rolin's friend was staying, and as she walked into the elegant hotel lobby realized it was a little too ornate for her tastes. Oh well, she was only staying for a couple of drinks, she'd survive. She found the gastropub where Rolin and his friend would be and heard Rolin's laugh first before she spotted them.

Rolin was his usual handsome self. Dressed business casual but comfortable — always so at ease within himself. And then Dorothy saw his companion and suddenly felt underdressed. The radiant woman sitting across from him wore a stunning black cocktail dress with a snow-white wrap. Her delicate bejeweled fingers held a crystal cocktail glass.

Not for ages had Dorothy been so conscious of her own height and hoped Rolin's petite friend wouldn't stand. She went on the offensive. "Rolin. Found you. And you must be Anjali? No, please don't get up." A server materialized, as if out of thin air and Dorothy pointed to Anjali's glass. "One of those please."

"Ann, this is Dorothy Dennehy. Dorothy – Anjali Varma. But she likes to be called Ann."

Ann put her glass down and clasped one of Dorothy's hands between both of hers. "Hello, Dorothy, I have heard so much about you from Rolin. I feel as if I already know you, and I'm so pleased to meet you."

"But Rolin seems to have kept you a secret, Ann." Dorothy kicked herself. The words once out sounded petty, and it wasn't her intent.

Ann's warm laugh caught her off-guard. Her jet-black eyes sparkled. "That's our Rolin, and what makes him a good lawyer. Never divulge anything not necessary."

Good, an opening Dorothy could use. "Yes, he did say you're a lawyer as well, and have known each other for a long time?"

When Ann glanced at Rolin to confirm the statement, Dorothy's stomach did a small flip. The look Ann gave Rolin spoke volumes. They had a special friendship, something Dorothy had no part of, and it left her disquieted and uneasy. What was wrong with her?

"Rolin frequented New York many times early in his career and our paths often crossed. Sometimes we were on opposite sides in the courtroom, but we stayed friends. Isn't that right?"

"We had multiple opportunities to flex our legal opinions, and maybe that's enough said about it." The teasing tone Rolin used with Ann was familiar to Dorothy.

"And what brings you to Portland then?" Dorothy didn't know how to quell the emotions rising in her. She wasn't jealous, was she? She had no claims, other than friendship, on Rolin, but this meeting wasn't turning out as she expected.

"A boring tax evasion case, on a corporate scale. Nothing as exciting as what Rolin used to specialize in. But enough about me. You're a private investigator? You must have so many interesting stories you could tell."

"Now then, Ann," said Rolin. "Like we lawyers, Dorothy respects the confidentiality of her clients."

"Yes, of course." She changed subjects and the genuine interest shown in her eyes was disarming as she asked, "How long have you lived in Portland?" Despite herself, Dorothy began to warm to the sincere friendliness of Anjali Varma's personality and by the time the evening ended, they were close to becoming friends.

"Dee, we'd love it if you joined us for dinner. What do you say?"

She hesitated. "Rolin, it's very kind of you, but I'm sure you two have lots to catch up on. I'm going to pass but thank you. I need to prepare, if I can, for a meeting with Sergeant Keleher first thing tomorrow, and be on my game."

"By the tone of your voice, you're no fan of this sergeant?" asked Ann.

"Let's say we haven't got off on the best foot. I hope to rectify it tomorrow, depending on why she wants to see me." Dorothy stood. "It was a pleasure to meet you, Ann. If time allows, maybe we can meet again before you leave Portland?" Dorothy surprised herself with the offer, but it was heartfelt. She did like her.

And judging by the smile on Rolin's face, it had been the right thing to say.

CHAPTER TWELVE

HB wasn't sure what he expected on his fact-finding mission to the winery. But he wanted to talk to as many of the employees as possible. His list had 7 names; Frisco Butler would have made the eighth. Ruts in the gravel driveway had pooled with water from overnight rain and he promised himself to hit a carwash after this visit. And then his favorite all-night diner for a decent breakfast.

Police presence was minimal, crime scene tape all but gone, so he hadn't been stopped. He pulled his car in behind a late model BMW, taking a moment to gather his thoughts before walking to the front door. A curtain moved, catching his eye.

He raised his hand to knock, but paused when he heard raised voices on the other side. Female and each trying to drown out the other. He hoped someone would hear him.

He shouldn't have been surprised when a uniformed officer opened the door. Xander Michelson was expecting him, and the officer let him pass.

"Sounds like a heated exchange in there?" HB pointed in the direction of the piercing vocal exchange.

"Been like that for about half an hour. Good luck."

HB followed the voices and stood in the doorway of a spacious living area. Two women, no, make that one woman and a teenager, stood face to face. The young girl would have to be Charlotte, and HB had no idea who her combatant was. But she was stunning. Darker skinned than Charlotte, her glossy black hair framed a model's face. She could be 30 or 45, hard to say. HB was no expert, but he'd seen some of Alanna's outfits and guessed this woman had a sizable clothing budget. Wait, this had to be the missing mother. Olivia St John-Rivard. Perfect timing.

The woman's face was inches from Charlotte's. HB would rather confront an armed attacker. He had no frame of reference for feuding females. If it weren't for the assignment to be here, he'd leave.

"Excuse me."

The tension between the two originated with the older woman, he guessed. But then the sullen faced girl wasn't helping as her mother demanded to know why there was no household staff. He tried again. "Excuse me!"

Two faces, united in their annoyance, turned in his direction. The older woman didn't speak, but her irate expression at being interrupted demanded he explain.

"Xander Michelson asked me to come. Is he here?"

Charlotte shot him a blank stare. And before the woman could take aim at him, he headed her off. "You must be Olivia St John-Rivard? I'm Holden Bartholomew. My boss and I have been looking for you."

"Fine, but we are in the middle of a conversation. If you wouldn't mind giving us five minutes to finish." She spoke to him as if he were one of the absent servants and pointed him in the direction of the hallway.

He backed out of the room, moved out of view, but not out of hearing. The mother picked up without missing a beat. "Again, why are there no staff to look after things around here? This place is a mess. I could do with something to eat. Airlines don't even offer peanuts anymore!" HB strained to hear a response from the daughter, but her reply was muffled.

"Don't mumble so. What did you say?"

"I said make your own coffee. If you can remember where the kitchen is. Dad and I don't need servants, like some people. We can take care of ourselves."

"Charlotte! What has happened to you? Why do you insist on looking like one of the walking dead? You were never interested in crystals and ... and psychic stuff. And you never spoke to me like that before."

"Before? Before what? Before you ran off and left me? Before my father was kidnapped or *before* someone died here?"

HB was ready to step back into the room, until he heard a sob and sniffles. Tears, he hated tears. He'd wait a couple more minutes.

At least the tears had a calming effect on Olivia St John-Rivard. She softened her voice as she spoke to her daughter. "You know I came as soon as I could. A kidnapping, and a death - I don't know how to cope!"

HB was surprised at the rage in Charlotte's voice. She wasn't going to be placated.

"Of course, you can't cope! Unbelievable. Nobody could find you! Uncle Xander didn't know what to do. Where were you?"

"I, I was in Houston, on ... holiday. I heard some investigator, or the police, doesn't matter which, were looking for me. Soon as I heard, I got the first plane here. About your father. You were the one who got the ransom note, right?"

HB thought her excuses didn't ring sincere and apparently neither did her daughter.

"Yeah, my birthday wasn't enough for you to be here, it took a kidnap to get your attention. I cannot wait to be 18 and be done with you!"

There were more sobs and then a final stab. "Glad Uncle Xander was here. At least he knows how to be more of a parent than you'll ever be. You'd better get your mommy act on for when the cops talk to you."

The exaggerated sigh from Oliva gave HB his cue to re-enter the scene. "Ladies, I appreciate this is a hard time, but I need to talk with Mr. Michelson."

Charlotte now aimed her venom at him. "Talk — *talk?* Someone should be out looking for my father and you want to talk!"

HB didn't react to the verbal attack. He was no shrink, but these two had no love lost between them. Of the two he might get more information from the daughter, if he could make a connection. Kids weren't his strong point though. Hell, why was he here again?

He'd try with the mother first. "Mrs. St John-Rivard? As I mentioned, my boss, Dorothy Dennehy and I were trying to locate you, so she'll be glad to know you're here now." He handed a business card to her.

"Give me one, too."

HB obliged and handed one to Charlotte. A start to making that connection, with any luck.

Oliva glanced at the card and tossed it into her purse. She started to light up a cigarette, but the glare from her daughter made her reconsider. She tossed her glossy mane and unpacked her social manners before moderating her tone with HB.

"Yes, of course, I came as soon as I heard. But I'm at a loss to understand why the police and a private investigator firm are involved. Don't the police take precedence? And what progress have they made? I will add whatever money I can to pay the ransom!"

The pretense at being in control dissolved, as Olivia collapsed into the overstuffed sofa and searched for a tissue. "This is just all too much. I don't know what to do!"

Movement in the doorway grabbed his attention. The officer who'd let him in walked into the room, accompanied by a detective he recognized from the precinct. Charlotte sniffed and tossed her head. "I bet you want to talk with her. My long-lost mother, the wonderful Olivia St John-Rivard."

HB exchanged a knowing look with the cop. But it was the detective who said, "Thank you, yes. Mrs. St John-Rivard, may we have a word? Here is fine."

"She's all yours. I'm outta here."

"I was just leaving too," said HB. No need for them to know the reason for his visit, other than Xander Michelson has asked to see him. "Say, Charlotte, can you tell me where your Mr. Michelson is?"

She shrugged. "Yeah, follow me." Then she turned back to face her mother. "And don't expect her to get either of you a coffee!"

As they left the house and headed toward another building on the property HB wasn't sure what they'd get from the mother. He'd like to have been a fly on the wall, but for now he'd focus on Michelson, and by extension this sulking, and rude, individual he was following.

They walked in silence for a few moments, their feet crunching on gravel. HB had no idea how to talk to this person, so decided to be direct. "You're not happy to see your mother. Lots of reasons I'm guessing."

"Not that it's any of your business but she was the one who left me - when I was just a kid."

HB knew what she meant and ignored the irony. "I'm aware. But I've been hired by your godfather, or uncle, to find your father. Quick question. Do you prefer I call him your uncle or your godfather?" As they walked toward the fermentation area where the barrels were kept, fresh tears flowed, and Charlotte turned her stricken face toward him. Crap, it wasn't that difficult of a question, was it?

"Why haven't the police found him yet? It's money they want - I say give it to them. I have some saved, too. I just want my dad back."

"Listen, Charlotte. I know this is really hard, but you have to be patient. I promise the cops are doing all they can to find him." HB had a flash of inspiration. "Tell me a bit about your dad, what he's like."

She looked at him, a frown replacing tears. "I never really thought about it. He's ... he's just my dad. Sometimes he won't let me do stuff or hang out with friends I like. And he works. A lot. Especially since my mom left and now that Uncle — ya, you can call him that — Xander's not here anymore. I wish he'd never left. He's always fun to be around. Plays, or used to, video games with me. I like that."

Interesting. The kid seemed to have more affection for Xander than her father, but maybe that wasn't unusual. What did he know? She wasn't yet done, gearing up for another attack on her mother, HB guessed.

"She's such a liar, too."

HB didn't interrupt her, and he waited for more. "For sure she came back earlier than she said. I don't know what her game is, but Uncle Xander better not get involved with her again."

So, she was aware of the affair and reason for the divorce. She wouldn't have been very old when everything fell apart. HB was beginning to think Charlotte's dislike of her mother was well-founded. He risked a question.

"What makes you think that?"

"I'm not stupid, you know. They think they can hide the way they look at each other. Gross."

HB didn't know how to comment on the observation. But he needed to learn more and didn't want Charlotte to realize she was ratting on the adults in her life. He needn't have worried, she was on a tear. "She left her phone out. Can you believe she doesn't put a lock on it? So, I scrolled through her text messages. Tons of them between her and Uncle Xander. Mushy stuff and she said she'd see him on the 18th -that's days ago, and the same day Dad disappeared. She wants me to think she's only just got here! Bitch. I wish she'd go back to wherever. Dad and I don't need her here." Her breath caught. "My dad will get found, right?"

An unfamiliar surge of something protective flashed over HB and he put his hand on her shoulder. "Charlotte, I'm not going to lie and promise something that might not happen. But I do promise the police, and my agency and I will do everything we can to find him."

Without warning, she wrapped her arms around him and hugged him. "Thank you for not treating me like a little kid."

He gently untangled her and found his voice was gruffer than he wanted. "Okay, got it, thanks. I guess you know a lot of the staff and crew who work around here?"

She nodded. Talking seemed to have calmed her down, with only an occasional hiccup interrupting.

"I ... I used to know most of the workers. I think there's only ever about eight or ten, but they change a lot. I used to love playing hide and seek when I was little. Lots of neat places to hide. I liked the big barrels, but Dad said it was off-limits. Sometimes the workers would play with me. Not so much now. Hide and seek is for babies anyway. Whatever."

HB was relieved the tears had stopped, but her mood rode in waves. He risked a more specific question. "Did you know Frisco Butler, then?"

She took a sharp intake of breath. "The one who's dead?" She shook her head. "I didn't like him. Besides, I don't hang out much here anymore. Schoolwork and stuff, you know." She looked at HB. "But this was an accident, right? It's not connected to my dad, is it?"

HB regarded her solemn face, a face streaked by a trail of tears. Still very much a child but facing unexpected and tough grown-up situations without much help.

"There is only so much I can tell you. I know you're old enough to understand it's an active investigation. You've seen cop shows, right? But I promise to tell you when there is anything I think you need to know, okay?"

Charlotte looked thoughtful. She wasn't such a bad kid - away from her mother at any rate. And then she totally changed the topic.

"You might guess I'm not a big fan of long names. What if I marry someone who also has a hyphen in their name! I bet you shorten yours, am I right?"

HB laughed at her for being so forthright. "You're right. I shorten Holden Bartholomew down to HB, which I bet you can understand."

Charlotte also laughed, and seemed more relaxed as they entered the barrel room. HB had never been inside the business end of winemaking before, and he was intrigued by what he saw. Row upon row of oak barrels, stacked 3 deep, on either side of a cavernous room with a concrete floor. The rows flanked a center space where two long tables and chairs took up residence. The temperature was cooler than outside. He saw yellow crime scene tape remained at one end of the rows farthest from where they stood. He wouldn't be allowed anywhere near the crime scene for now.

"That's for parties and special events," said Charlotte. "Gets done up with tablecloths and fancy dishes."

"Nice," he said. "I need a tour."

She laughed. "Over there, through that door, is where they bottle the wine. That's probably where you'll find anyone who's working." She paused. "It does seem kind of quiet here."

Sure enough as they entered the bottling process area, HB could see work had come to a standstill. A handful of workers hovered around Xander Michelson, peppering him with questions.

Before they were spotted, HB needed Charlotte's help. "Okay, this is what I can tell you. I'd really like to speak with your uncle and his staff before the cops throw me out. We don't always see eye-to-eye, if you know what I mean?"

"Back to those cop shows, right. You guys should work together, you know?"

HB shrugged. "In a perfect world, maybe. But you get it?" She nodded.

He smiled. "I knew there was something about you I liked. Oh, your uncle sees you. Remember what I said, okay?"

"I remember what you promised."

"Charlotte!" Xander ran over and hugged his goddaughter. He broke the embrace with her and looked at HB. His eyes beseeching HB for some answers. "Have you any news?"

Charlotte answered. "My mother has arrived, if you can call that news."

"She's here? Right. We need to let her know everything is being done to find your father."

Charlotte's bad temper resurfaced. "She knows. I've seen her and I'm in no hurry to play mother-daughter. Anyway, she's with the police now, so she can use her charms on them. Guess they'll talk about Frisco Butler. That his death is suspicious. Words they use for murder you know. I watch lots of cop shows." She shot a smug look at HB.

Xander turned to HB. "So, I take it no news from you then. Do you need anything from me?" He rubbed his neck. "Ah, you did mention wanting to speak with the employees. Not sure the cops will let you so now's your chance while they're busy with Olivia. I've told them to talk to you, hold nothing back. Likewise, the same for the police if, or when, they're interviewed. Oh, and make sure you speak to Mandy Peterson. She works in the office. She's bound to know as much as anyone and knows how this place works. She's likely privileged to more news, or gossip, than I am."

HB quickly assessed the six people before him. He'd need some time to talk to all of them. "Anything, sir, you can do to delay the cops, within reason, would be appreciated, if you get my drift."

"Of course, I'll do what I can. I'll leave you to it. Come on Charlotte. We have things to discuss with your mother."

Charlotte offered her uncle a churlish face, but waved at HB and provided a hint of a smile. "Catch you later, HB."

Connection made.

HB moved farther into the scrupulously pristine bottling area, surprised how clean and orderly it was. Four men and two women stood with curious, or fearful, expressions as they waited for him to speak. He should have brought another notebook. Instead, he asked, and got, permission to record his conversations with each of them.

He would have preferred to speak to each person in private, but there wasn't time, so the next half hour was spent asking questions about the winery, about Etienne Rivard, Xander Michelson and looking for any comments pertaining to the investigation. Some comments were guarded, and he might have to talk to one or two employees later.

He'd have a lot of notes to type up later for a summary to Dorothy.

"I appreciate taking your time away from your jobs, and please make sure you don't change any of what you've told me should you be interviewed by the police. At the end of the day, both the police and my agency are working to find Etienne Rivard and possibly determine what happened to Mr. Butler. Now if someone can point me in the direction of the office, I have one last person to see. Mandy Peterson."

The office where she worked was in the annex alongside the main house. It also served as the public face of Michard Estates. Brochures and a showcase of sample wine bottles highlighted a small reception area. A large whiteboard showed upcoming events.

At the end of a small hallway was a sign indicating deliveries. A pair of glass doors, closed, led to offices. Etienne's name was on the first door. The second door was nameless-maybe it had been Xander's and now vacant?

Mandy Peterson's domain appeared to encompass reception and a glassed-in cubicle off to one side.

HB thought the area, while not overly large, was well laid out and made good use of the space. He noted the office equipment was current and top of the line. Impressive.

She hadn't looked up when he entered, and he tapped gently on the glass wall. "Mandy Peterson? I believe you were told to expect me. Holden Bartholomew - I'm working on the disappearance of Etienne Rivard."

As she stood to acknowledge his presence, his phone chirped. He held up one finger, glanced at the caller ID, and apologized. "Sorry, I need to take this."

He walked to the other side of the room. "Boss."

"Anything to report? I'm with Detective Keleher and we're discussing how we can help with this investigation so if you have anything to share ...?"

He lowered his voice, not the greatest time to provide a status update. "I'm at the winery now and in the office. Still information gathering. You'll be pleased to know I've met Olivia St John-Rivard, who has apparently just returned. I'm sure that's known by your friend as well. She arrived this morning. Daughter Charlotte not too happy I'll get back with a full recap later today."

"Thanks, I'll let Detective Keleher know Olivia has been found."

"Well, the cops are with her now so I'm sure she knows already."

"Likely, but I will confirm. I'll meet you at the *Aye* this afternoon."

"Aye, Aye captain!"

"Is that your attempt at humor, HB?"

HB suppressed a sarcastic response and clicked off. He turned to Mandy Peterson. He hoped anything she'd heard wouldn't affect his questions to her.

CHAPTER THIRTEEN

Dorothy closed her phone and spoke to Sergeant Shelby Keleher. "I hope you believe me now when I say my team and I want the same thing as yours – the safe return of Etienne Rivard. He's been missing for nearly a week. I don't need to tell you that's not a good thing. If Butler was working alone, well ..."

When Dorothy had arrived at the Sergeant's office less than an hour ago, she wasn't sure what to expect. That Keleher had requested the meeting could mean she was going to warn Dorothy and her team away from the investigation, or — slim chance — she'd allow them to partner. She was determined to keep her options open and see how Keleher wanted to play the meeting.

Even though Keleher was on a temporary assignment and using Reg Pierson's office, she'd removed anything personal of Reg's. Commendations, framed newspaper articles and the one photo Dorothy always liked. Pierson as a kid, holding up his prize catch of the day. A fish almost as big as the eight-year-old in the picture. And a smile Dorothy hadn't seen much in recent memory. The job was stressful, and she hoped Reg was doing well whatever reason given for his leave.

In contrast, Keleher's space was sterile, evoking an authoritarian air. A mood which had infiltrated the whole department. Still, Dorothy vowed not to judge - at least not until she had a chance to learn what might lay beneath the expressionless face of Shelby Keleher.

Keleher's index finger tapped the desk. Dorothy thought it might be an unconscious habit because Keleher seemed unaware of it. When the tapping stopped, Keleher spoke. "I'm well aware of the situation. Officers have been pulled from other departments to help in the search. We will find him."

Dorothy bit her tongue. Yes, he probably would be found, but would he still be alive? This was wasting time, but Keleher was in charge and Dorothy put a lid on her impatience.

"I deal in facts, Ms. Dennehy. And only have your word what you say is true. Although," she paused, "anyone I've spoken to concerning you and your team have given me nothing to doubt your integrity."

Okay, then. Talk about a back-handed compliment. "Thank you. I appreciate the feedback. You may be aware I've taken a step back from investigating. HB," she touched her phone, "is in charge and he has my full confidence. Likewise, I never doubt his integrity. But I do seem to have become more involved than I'd intended."

Keleher nodded. "You owe him because he saved your life in Detroit."

Dorothy didn't care for the implication. "I owe him nothing, other than my loyalty and friendship. He was doing his job and doing it well." But she was intrigued that the Sergeant had checked into the case.

Keleher cleared her throat. "I apologize. This didn't sound the way I intended. I have met HB ..."

She was interrupted by a knock at her door. "Sorry Sarge, we've got that background information you wanted."

Keleher waved the officer in and took the paperwork from her hands. "Thank you, Wyatt. Close the door on the way out."

Dorothy waited to see if more on HB was forthcoming, but the interruption had brought a change in direction.

Keleher quickly scanned the pages and looked at Dorothy.

"Olivia St John-Rivard. Did HB give you any kind of take on her in that call?"

Dorothy proceeded with caution. This was an opening, and she didn't want to blow it. "He didn't want to be overheard, so no, not really. Only to say her daughter, Charlotte, didn't seem thrilled to have her mother return."

Keleher nodded. "She's been out of the picture for about two years. Enjoying a good life lots of money can provide. Her family has money, and influence, in Manhattan.

"They don't have so much money these days." Dorothy gave her an overview of what Rolin had learned. "It might help to verify exactly when this woman arrived back in the area. There seems to be a disconnect. I gather from HB she's not being upfront, with her daughter at least, of when she came back home. Especially if you think she's involved?" Dorothy brought out her notebook and pen. "Do you mind?"

"No. I'll confirm her arrival and let you know." Keleher took a breath. "Right. This is how it will work. Your team obviously has ways to find information we don't have access to."

"And vice versa. And I think you can call me Dorothy."

"Of course." Keleher dismissed Dorothy's comment. "You agree there will be times we cannot, legally, share what we may learn. You and your team, on the other hand, do have a similar legal obligation to keep us advised of any new information. Or risk obstruction of justice charges. Am I clear on this?"

"I agree and wouldn't ask anything more of the department." Dorothy flipped over to a clean page. "Now, can we talk about St John-Rivard? It sounds as if you suspect, or suspected, her involvement with the kidnapping."

Keleher continued with her summation. "As with most crimes of this nature, those closest to the family are always under scrutiny. We thought her alibi for the time of the kidnapping was air tight. But maybe not so much. And before you provided background financial information, we had found no monetary reason she'd want to extort funds. May or may not be significant. By all accounts, and by accounts, I mean social media as well, she was more than glad to be free of Portland, husband Etienne, and the lover, Xander Michelson. Her family, as I said, is — or was — wealthy and she's part of that society. What I don't get is how she could cut all ties with her daughter. That's cold."

Dorothy filed away the last comment. If Keleher could recognize that behavior in St John-Rivard, maybe her own frosty exterior was a front.

Over the next twenty minutes they compared notes. Keleher shared that the autopsy revealed blunt force trauma to the back of Butler's head, not merely the result of a fall on concrete. He had been murdered. Dorothy wasn't surprised by the news but kept that to herself. The department had also discovered Kevin Butler – Frisco – was pretty much a drifter. Track record of petty crimes. Shoplifting, and trespassing. But had recently escalated to dealing drugs and seemed to be settled in the area likely due to a steady clientele. Dorothy skimmed over the shared rap sheet. "He stole a dog?"

"With the intent of holding it for ransom. Dog ran away first."

They laughed but the implication of extortion wasn't lost on either of them. Dorothy commented, "So he ventured into the big times with a kidnap of his employer?"

"And now he's dead. How the hell do we find the victim?" Keleher was frustrated. "Although, murder implies an accomplice. Because I don't think it's a coincidence."

"And could mean Etienne is still alive and the ransom is still needed."

"Exactly. So, we're concentrating on known associates. Butler's track record doesn't make me think he could be the mastermind. He must have an accomplice. And, this is where your team could come in - Dorothy."

"I'll get HB on this right away. He may have picked up some info by talking to the staff at Michard Estates. Which, of course, I will share with you at once."

Keleher tidied up the paperwork, and while focused on her desk asked about HB. "So, I mentioned earlier I have met HB. You've known him long?"

The tone of her voice had changed, and Dorothy recognized a different question of interest about her right-hand man. "Yes. A couple of decades or more. It's actually he and my father who have the longest friendship. When I first started my agency, Dad recommended him to me, and I've never looked back." She hesitated before adding. "He can be hard to get to know, but if he counts you as a friend, you couldn't ask for better."

"I see. No, ah, romantic interest between you two?"

"What? HB! As if. Sorry, no. And now I apologize for how that sounded. I know he'd go to the ends of the earth for me, as I would for him, but that's it. He's pretty much a loner in that department. His ... his one love, that I know of, died in a tragic explosion long before I knew him and that's it."

"Understood. Not wanting to pry, you understand, but I like to have a sense of who I work with."

But more about HB than her, Dorothy assumed. Interesting to say the least.

Dorothy stood. "I think we've covered what we need to. As I said, HB will have a report for me later and I will forward everything he's learned on to you. I'm pleased we have found a way to work together, Sergeant Keleher. And I promise my team and I will not get in your way."

Keleher walked over to the door, holding her hand on it for a moment. "In front of my team, call me Sergeant, but like this, I'm Shelby." The door opened.

Dorothy left the building, amused by the contradiction Keleher — Shelby — presented, but relieved they'd found a way to work together.

Now she could focus on whatever HB had dug up at the winery.

She returned to her Jeep and saw she'd missed a call from Lucas. She quickly connected with him. "Hope I'm not interrupting you slicing into a heart or liver?"

Her cousin Lucas laughed. "Not yet. Almost ready to look at a brain though. Interested?"

"Hard pass, but thanks. You called me, anything interesting?"

"One sec." She could hear muffled voices and then Lucas was back online. "Sorry, we have an intern with us today and she nearly put the brain in with the lungs. Stopped her just in time."

"Nice. Thanks for sharing. Think I'll pass on lunch now. What's up."

He lowered his voice. "Okay, you didn't hear this from me, but the complete autopsy on Kevin Butler shows blunt force trauma, so ..."

"He was murdered. Yes, I just learned that from the Sergeant. Anything else?"

"Saving the best for last, cuz. Did Keleher also mention the physical evidence we found on the body?"

"Go on."

"Shards of a wine bottle, and wine. Implied the bottle was full and therefore made a good weapon. Plus, something we haven't been able to identify yet. A fragment of a rubber-based material, red in color. All this information went to the police."

"Brilliant, Lucas. Thank you. I didn't know about the bottle shards and whatever the red material is. If you find out, let me know."

"You've got it. Oh, crap. Now she's mixing formaldehyde with stomach contents! Bye!"

CHAPTER FOURTEEN

HB turned to speak to Mandy Peterson. She looked up from her computer and greeted him with a scowl. A scowl which detracted from her blonde good looks. Was she annoyed because he'd taken a call? Or something else? The call hadn't taken that long.

"The office is closed." She promptly turned her attention back to her computer.

HB was in for a hard sell. "I'm sorry to interrupt your workday Ms. Peterson but as I started to explain I've been hired by Xander Michelson with regards to the disappearance of Etienne Rivard. Am I correct to assume you've worked here long enough to know Mr. Michelson?"

He handed her a business card. "This is the company I work for — private investigations." No response. Just what he needed after dealing with a truculent teenager, although Charlotte might have more manners - barely. Finally, the petulant young woman faced him. He wasn't good at guessing ages. She could be anywhere from twenty to thirty. And the steel piercings in her nose and eyebrow were not unique to any age these days. He didn't see the attraction and tore his gaze away. He tried a different tactic. Maybe she was grumpy because it was the weekend. "Do you always work on a Saturday?"

"Seriously? No, I don't, and to set the record straight, I had plans for today and then I was summoned to work because of this fiasco. Tom Romano — he's kind of in charge when

Etienne's not around — said all employees had to talk to the cops. But Xander is back, too, and thinks he's the one in charge. I'd rather take orders from Tom. Anyway, so here I am."

Right, and the kidnapping was an inconvenience to her plans. What was wrong with people? He couldn't be bothered trying to connect with her.

"A kidnapping is serious business. Aren't you concerned for your employer? Your paycheck will likely stop if he's not found."

At last, a comment that hit the mark. She showed some interest. "Why?"

If he had to explain to her, he'd give up. But he sure had a question. Who the hell hired this person? Customer service, or logical thought, wasn't her strong point. He sighed inwardly. "I'm just trying to find out what I can, to see if it helps. To see if you can shed any light on his kidnapping. How did the staff feel about him? Any grudges or complaints?"

"Can you slow down with the questions? I'm not a robot. Of course, I'm upset Etienne's been kidnapped but it's nothing to do with me if that's what you're thinking. Maybe he should treat his employees better, know what I mean? Not everyone here's always on the right side of Etienne Rivard!"

HB noted the familiarity of first name use. He briefly recalled how long it had been before he was comfortable calling Dorothy by her first name and not Ms. Dennehy. Kids these days.

He dug a little deeper into his shrinking supply of patience. "Sorry, I don't know what you mean. How about an example? Are you one of those not on the right side? You seem angry."

Mandy Peterson rose from behind her desk, giving HB the once over before speaking. They were about the same height, so they were eye to eye. He couldn't gauge her response to his questions but was surprised when she said, "He rejected me, right? I thought he liked me, you know - liked me. Made me think this job," she waved be-ringed fingers across her desk, "would be only for a while."

"And how long have you been working here?"

"Almost two years, started just before Xander left. So anyway, at first it was all good. He'd buy me coffee and even took me out for dinner once. And what if I made a couple of billing errors? I've never worked in an office before."

HB began to put the pieces together but let her continue. "I thought we were, like, a thing, you know? And then the next time I was late for work, he was mad. Sheesh. It's hard to get up when it's dark outside, right?"

HB bit back a response and stayed on topic. "So was his behavior inappropriate toward you?"

"Huh? Oh, you mean did he want sex? Most bosses do, so I guess he would be the same. But no, never did."

HB thought if her pout grew any larger her chin would disappear. "And you were disappointed then?"

"Well, that's where the good gifts and bonuses come from, don't they? And now he's probably dead. And like you said, I won't even get paid for this week. Not a surprise, I guess. He was starting to gaslight me. Bad reviews, warnings, stuff like that. I think he wanted to fire me."

HB contemplated what he'd heard. Was Mandy Peterson putting on an act or was she as immature as she appeared? Either way, the cops would find it interesting when she talked with them. She definitely had a motive to be involved with the kidnap, and evidence suggested Frisco couldn't have acted alone. But he wasn't going to comment on anything she'd said about Rivard's perceived, or otherwise, intent. That was a minefield he wasn't prepared to walk through.

"I appreciate your candor, thank you. Now, you said others weren't happy with the way Etienne treated them. Was Frisco Butler one of them? Did he have a grudge against his employer?"

Mandy slumped in her seat and looked ready to cry. "What do you want from me? I told you about Etienne and he probably treated the other employees the same. He discards you when you're not needed anymore. As for that creep Frisco Butler. Never could stand him. Had it coming to him. Not well liked from what I've heard."

"I see. Before I forget, who handles hiring around here?"

"It was up to Etienne, especially after Xander left. That had been his responsibility. When I first started Etienne mentioned it might be a role I could take on, but he never brought it up again, even after Xander left."

He thought that was no surprise but left it alone and focused on Frisco Butler. "Can you tell me what you heard? Any information would really help the investigation."

Mandy stood and walked around her desk to the open door. Her arms were crossed, and the belligerent look on her face was back.

"Listen, I think I've told you enough. I don't know you and I thought it was the cops I was to speak to today. You should go."

"I'm leaving, relax. The cops will likely be here to speak with you later today, so don't leave, okay? They're doing all they can to find Etienne. Right now, they're at the house, speaking with his wife, um, I mean ex-wife."

Mandy dropped her arms, her face diffused with red blotches. "That bitch. What's she doing back? Nothing was the same around here after Xander left but I was so glad to see the back of her. I bet she's looking for an opportunity to fix herself up. Do they think she's involved? I doubt it, she comes from loads of money. In New York, I think."

HB wondered if he'd need an anti-venom shot after that outburst. The Rivards couldn't both be that distasteful, could they? He hadn't got the same sense from the other staff concerning Etienne. He understood the ax Mandy Peterson had to grind, but why the hatred toward the ex?

The window of opportunity to gain more from Mandy Peterson slammed shut with the arrival of the detective and officer HB had seen earlier. They weren't happy to see him talking with their next line of enquiry.

"We're here to speak with Mandy Peterson." The detective looked over at the stone-faced young woman. "I assume that's you. And you," he glared at HB, "may leave."

HB wanted to wish them well but was taken aback by the instant change in Mandy Peterson's attitude. She smiled at him. "I have your card, HB. Maybe we can talk more sometime? I know all about wines. We could have a wine tasting. Stop at the gift shop on your way out and try our Pinot Noir."

What the hell? Women. First Charlotte and then this ... this ... anomaly. Maybe Dorothy could explain it. He'd never understood the way women's minds worked. Maybe it was better he didn't. Unless Mandy Peterson had more information to share?

"Good luck, gentlemen. I'll leave you to it."

He turned and walked away, completely baffled by the pleasant, and business-like, voice Mandy Peterson was using on the police. The gift shop came into view and HB shrugged to himself.

Ten minutes later, he put the bottle of Michard Estates Pinot Noir on the seat beside him and began the drive back to the marina and home base. He and Dorothy needed to compare notes right away, and the wine wouldn't hurt. Etienne Rivard had been gone for 5 days now. With Frisco Butler dead the clock was ticking on finding him alive.

CHAPTER FIFTEEN

The October sunshine was fading fast as Dorothy approached the *Aye*. She was early and didn't hesitate before going aboard. This was HB's domain now, but it had been her refuge for a long time as well. A stiff breeze coming off the water whipped her hair about her face. HB insisted she keep a key, which she rarely used, even though he continued to tell her she was welcome anytime.

She'd brought a couple of subs prepared back at the bar and set about putting on a pot of coffee.

While it brewed, she let her mind drift back. Sometimes she stopped the memories of time spent with Paul when they surfaced, but when it was quiet like this, and reminders were all around, she gave in. She still missed him, and her heart ached at times, but now thoughts of him brought her comfort and a sense of peace. And she'd always be grateful for the time — the time far too short — that they'd had.

The sunshine disappeared, replaced by dark clouds which hastened an early evening. A distant rumble concerned her that HB would get caught in the rain. She switched on the lights and spread her notes out on the table. She'd also brought along a copy of today's Portland Tribune. Keleher wouldn't be amused.

Local Cops Not up to Speed on Kidnapping filled the headline.

Footsteps on the deck outside announced HB's arrival. He came inside and shook off a jacket spattered with rain. "Gonna be a downpour any minute, boss. Coffee? I've got this as well." He held up the wine bottle.

"Ah, an offering from the source I assume. Maybe later if that's okay?"

HB put the bottle to one side. "I definitely need this, or something stronger. Women!" He offered an apology. "But not you, Boss. I mean the ones I met today."

Dorothy laughed. "You had an enlightening day?"

"Not the word I'd use "He spied the hefty sandwich. "Oh, tell me that's turkey and bacon?"

"See, you are a good detective. Let's eat and compare notes."

Dorothy found HB's observations of the women he'd met at the winery revealing. He seemed to have made a connection with Charlotte, which could be useful. Especially her revelation, and assessment, of her own mother. But Mandy Peterson raised flags. "Let's have Jordan Klein do some background checking on her. Maybe tail her for a bit when she leaves the winery. None of the other staff gave you any concern?"

"Not really. Kind of neutral comments from 'I like working here; no issues'; to 'Etienne is a good boss'. They all seemed genuinely concerned for his well-being. There's only six in the production end of things. You've met their driver, Carter Hayes. The other five divide their time between bottling and taking care of the fields. Michelson was responsible for staff hiring. He must have had an off day when hiring Butler, but Rivard wasn't much better in his hiring pick of Mandy Peterson. Everyone agreed Kevin Butler wasn't a good team player."

"Or what you saw today with Mandy Peterson, may all be a front. There's only her word, or her interpretation, regarding him. I may have to meet her myself, or perhaps you can follow up with her if she's interested in you?" Dorothy crumpled up the wrapper from her now gone sandwich. "Which reminds me. Shelby Keleher. My radar says she might be more than a little interested in you as well. You know we women love a man who could be a challenge."

"A challenge? Nice one. But Keleher?" He flipped through some notes, trying to appear uninterested, Dorothy thought. "What makes you say that?"

Dorothy didn't speak but tapped the side of her nose. Then she grew serious. "See the headline?"

He grunted. "Well, it has been a few days. If Butler was acting alone, Rivard could be dead. Hate to say it, because the kid, Charlotte, will be even more of a mess. And I don't get a good feeling from her mother. More than just rich and entitled."

"But here's the thing, Butler probably wasn't acting alone." Dorothy gave HB the autopsy information.

He nodded when she mentioned the fragment of leather. "I have a good hunch I know what it is, boss."

"Which is?"

"Tell Lucas to look at it again and think boxing glove. Lucas doesn't have to say where he got the tip from, right?"

Dorothy was on the same page. "No, he does not, but you're thinking Xander?"

"Points that way, boss, doesn't it?"

Dorothy's phone buzzed. "It's Rolin. Hi. I'm with HB on the *Aye* – do you need me behind the bar?"

"No, it's all good here. But I just heard something interesting via Ann you might find valuable for your investigation."

Damn, it was all good until he said 'Ann'. Then that tiny little anxiety worm inched closer to her heart. Focus, girl. "Great. We're almost done here. I'll be back to the bar in about an hour. HB will come, too."

HB looked up at the mention of his name, and Dorothy told him they'd both be heading over. "And getting soaked by the looks of things." Rain teemed down and lights of the marina shimmered and wavered through the streams of water running down the windows of the *Aye*.

"Back to work," said Dorothy, and then added, "The wine will have to wait for another time. Not like we don't carry the brand behind the bar."

In short order, HB gave Dorothy enough information to forward to Keleher, in addition to her own thoughts.

The umbrella HB offered Dorothy wasn't much help when the rain decided to turn sideways. The wind had picked up and encouraged them to hurry the short distance from the *Aye* to the welcome warmth of Maxwell's Bar and Grill.

Saturday evening and the place was full. At least none of the staff had begged off for the night. Well, why would they? Best tips were Saturday night, but they were earned. Both Dorothy and Rolin worked hard to promote a healthy and respectful workplace. It seemed to be paying off. They hadn't had to hire any new staff for a few months. Social media reviews were consistently high, for food and service.

HB and Dorothy shook off as much water as they could and headed for the bar. As they moved closer Dorothy watched

Rolin. He was so at ease behind the bar. His smile was infectious and regular customers knew they'd be treated well. She was aware she'd left it all to him the past few days and hoped this case would soon wrap up so she could get back there with him. They made a good team.

He caught sight of them and waved them around to the far end of the bar. "I know we don't like to do this, but you are part owner," said Rolin as he removed Reserved placards from two bar stools. "However, the tips I've missed out on holding these seats for both of you. I may have to ask for a raise."

HB fished a five-dollar bill from his pocket. "Where's your tip jar?"

They laughed, and Rolin poured a glass of red for Dorothy and pulled a pint for HB. He turned and made himself a bourbon, neat. "Cheers, my friends."

They clinked glasses and HB turned to look at the packed room. "Max knew what he was doing when he let you guys take over. Look at this place!"

Dorothy knew the glow of contentment she felt wasn't solely due to the red wine. She was at home here and with two of her favorite people. Life was good. But there was still business to deal with.

"You said you have something of interest for us?"

"Yes, Dee. I haven't forgotten." He winked at her and emptied his glass. "So, Ann called me from the airport. She's on her way home. But through her far reaching financial and legal grapevine, she heard Olivia St John-Rivard's family may be in more serious financial distress than we thought."

Dorothy focused on the financial news rather than the small tingle of happiness she felt when hearing Ann had left. "How bad?"

"Obviously I don't know all the details, nor would Ann reveal them, but let's say it may be no coincidence Olivia St John-Rivard has returned. Might be no more room at the St John family home for her these days. The family have three properties in the New York area, all of them are up for sale - hoping to beat foreclosure action."

Dorothy sipped at her wine and considered the news. "Well, looks like the returning ex also has a motive to be involved with a kidnapping, doesn't it?"

CHAPTER SIXTEEN

Saturday's rain had given way to a warm and sunny October Sunday. It meant Michard Estates could expect to be busy with tourists, and locals, looking for something different to do. Taking in the scenery and checking out the shelves in the gift shop for a new wine to try.

Jordan Klein was grateful for another chance to prove his worth, when HB assigned him the chance to do a recon on the winery in general and Mandy Peterson in particular. He'd tried again to apologize for his error in judgment with the expense account. But HB had dismissed it, gruffly. Only saying this might be his chance to put the past in the past. Jordan was keen to make things right this time.

He parked in one of the few remaining spots and grabbed his camera from the seat beside him. He had an idea of sorts how to play this, but as HB always said, be prepared to be flexible and think on your feet!

He'd done a little research on the wine-making business and knew this was harvest time. There'd likely be a few migrant workers to supplement the regular staff in order to harvest the grapes off the vines. The tourists milling about might not be aware of the kidnapping, although the local papers had broken the story. Or maybe they did, and these were curiosity seekers anxious to embellish the account of their day at the winery to family and friends. In any event the temporary sign advising tours had been canceled would surely raise questions.

Jordan tended to be soft spoken, and personable. Women of his grandmother's age wanted to mother him - it was his sincerity that rang true with them. His long straggly hair might come in handy today. HB shared with Jordan it was because of his personality he felt he'd be perfect to act as a tourist, easily fading into the background when needed. When they'd met up earlier that morning, HB had provided details on the case, and a rough suggestion as to what was needed. "Basically, a fresh set of eyes, on the winery of course. But I got real mixed signals from Mandy Peterson. She worked there yesterday, so chances are she'll be there again today" He gave Jordan his assessment of the young office assistant.

Jordan had shaken his head. "She sounds immature at best, and psychotic at worst. Should be fun. Oh, say, I'm cleared to partake in wine tasting if need be? I respect Quail's guidelines on not drinking on the job, but ... "

"Use your initiative, and discretion, Jordan. I'll make an exception. They only give you an ounce or two so use common sense. And if you buy some to look legit, yes, you can put it on your expenses."

Jordan grinned. "Cool. Thanks, man. I'll keep track, record it on my expense account. You can count on it."

"And while we're talking about recording, maybe act like a tourist and take a few pictures of your surroundings. No one will suspect you're taking photos of people coming and going instead of the scenery, right? And remember, for now, the cops don't know you work for us. I'd like to keep you low profile for as long as possible. But if you get made, cooperate with them. We need to stay on good terms."

Jordan left HB, pumped at this new assignment. Too bad he was no fan of wine. Red, white, good or bad, and hoped it wouldn't be problematic. Now if this were a brewery instead? Oh, well, he could suffer in silence. It was his job.

Jordan had arrived at the winery the same time a minibus was parking. He watched in amusement as eight or ten older women spilled out, determined on the direction they were taking. He guessed they'd been here before. Think on your feet, that's what HB said. He repeated it to himself as he walked over to be the last in their line. He tapped the shoulder in front of him. "Excuse me, is this the line to sample a good Pinot? You ladies appear to know your way around here. Visited before?"

A shorter, sixty something lady with tight gray curls turned and smiled at Jordan. "That we have, Sunshine, many times. It's our book club, you see. We manage to come a couple of times a year. You can't beat a good Pinot Noir - pairs well with most murders." Her comment was met with giggles from her friends. Jordan had become their center of attention. He smiled and let her continue. "And this estate makes one of the best. Award winning you know. We always buy a case to have at our Christmas get together."

"What a coincidence. I'm here doing research for a book I'm writing. Maybe I could take a few pictures with you and your book club members?"

A ripple of excitement ran through the group. The lineup was forgotten as they encircled their new-found, book-writing, friend. Jordan hoped he hadn't gone overboard, and would need to reign this in. HB needed him to stay low profile, this was going south fast.

"How about a couple of pictures, ladies? Stand over this way." He grouped them together with wine barrels as the backdrop. What they weren't aware of was the fact Jordan was not focusing on them, instead snapping pictures of car license plates.

Kate Murphy introduced herself as president of the book club and Jordan worked hard to deflect questions about his own name. The more pictures he took of the group, the less interested they were in him. He hoped they'd never learn most of the pictures didn't feature them at all.

He fended off questions about the book he was supposed to be writing as his thesis on the winemaking industry.

Kate was bursting to ask, "I do hope you will be using our picture in your... what did you call it?"

"Well, my manuscript will be used as my thesis for the college classes I'm taking. Maybe I'll publish it later. We'll see what my professors think of it. Oh, look. I think you need to get back in line now or miss your chances."

Like a small flock of chirping birds, they turned as one to move toward their target. The full to bursting shelves of Michard Estates wine, and a table set up for wine tasting.

Off to one side, stood a young, and attractive blonde, chatting with customers. She matched the description HB had given him of Mandy Peterson. Likely needing the overtime for a Sunday. He'd circle back around to her after he'd explored the grounds first.

***

No one stopped him as he wandered the property, although he did notice the police presence. It didn't seem a concern for anyone. He hoped to be pegged as another tourist, but he'd stick to his story of writing a story about wine making if he was asked why he was taking so many pictures.

He found it odd though, that the winery would be open and didn't think the police would appreciate strangers wandering around. But then, maybe they had the same thought. Open for business could mean the kidnapper might be nearby and they were on the watch, just like him. The thought made him realize he was also vulnerable as a suspicious person, and he'd need to avoid any police interaction. He chanced a quick look at the buildings and didn't notice any security cameras, but that didn't mean they weren't there. Watching him.

He wasn't sure what he was looking for, anything of interest was probably happening in the house, but HB wanted him to be thorough and the volume of pictures he'd taken would prove that. He turned back and returned to the gift shop. Fortunately, the ladies had disappeared. Mandy Peterson stood by the wine sampling table and turned toward him with an all-business smile.

"Care for a taste?"

His charm came to the fore. "Maybe. You're not going to believe this, but wine's not really my thing. I was passing, saw the sign for wine tasting and thought why not? Family dinner tonight and here's a chance to up my game and pretend to be knowledgeable with a good bottle of red. What do you recommend?"

Mandy giggled and reached out to tap his wrist. Jordan wondered at the lack of professionalism. HB was probably right; this chick was all over the map. Especially after she lowered her voice to answer him. "Me neither, but those in the know say this Pinot Noir is the best. It's well known - if their advertising is to be believed. Here, try some."

Jordan sipped at the wine trying not to show his dislike for the red liquid. "I guess I'll take a bottle." As she completed the purchase transaction, he tried some small talk. "So, if you don't like wine either, doesn't that interfere with your job? I mean, how do you like working here? A couple of friends are looking for part time work, something like this could be good. Are they hiring by chance?"

Mandy looked around her to see who was watching and spoke quietly. "A job's a job, right? No way I'll be making this my lifetime career. You must be aware the owner has been kidnapped. Or do you think police patrol all the wineries in the area? They've been here for days. So, I'd say your friends are out of luck right now."

"Kidnapped! No way. Oh wait, I did see something online, but didn't clue into the connection here." He deliberately held eye contact with her. "Must be my lucky day you're open today, although I'd have thought business would be closed? Is there a reason why the place is open?"

His attempt at flirting seemed to hit the mark when Mandy tilted her head and pouted at him. "No kidding. Business as usual we were told. One of the former owners has shown up, and took right over, as if he'd never left." She glanced around and crooked her finger at him to lean in closer. "Actually, the guy was fired, truth be told. Weird he'd want to help out don't you think? So, I guess he's the one who decided we stay open. Like, what if we, that is me, was really upset at him being kidnapped, and maybe even dead! You don't know."

Jordan offered sympathy for her situation. "Yeah, some bosses. All that matters is the bottom line. Like employees aren't people too, with feelings."

Mandy sniffed. "But see, the one kidnapped - he is the boss."

"Oh, didn't realize, sorry. Not just the owner then? He's actually a hands-on employer?"

The sniff grew louder. "I might never see him again."

Oh, brother, if she started crying, Jordan was done. "Listen, it doesn't look too busy in here right now. Can you take a break - catch your breath?"

She perked up at the suggestion, finally offering a smile and kept her eyes locked on him. Her disloyal comments and whole manner didn't sit well with him and made him uneasy. More than ever, he felt HB's take on her was accurate. She ran hot and cold at the drop of a hat. An act? Or her true personality?

"You're sweet. How about that table over there in the sunshine? Ten minutes? I'll need to see to a couple of customers who just came in. By the way, my name's Mandy" She tapped her name tag. "I'll grab us coffees, okay? We don't do anything fancy though. Black, or white? Your coffee, I mean." She giggled again and followed up with a coy look. "You haven't told me your name?"

Jordan thought fast, trying to keep up with her mood changes was distracting. "Dan, you can call me Dan. And I'll take my coffee black, thanks."

She tilted her head, smiled, and turned her attention to wallet-producing customers.

Jordan moved back outside, glad of fresh air. He headed toward the picnic table she'd pointed out. She soon joined him, sitting beside him, rather than opposite. Too close for Jordan's comfort. He couldn't get any definite information from her, other than her general distaste for Kevin Butler and her complaints about having to work while Etienne was still missing. He found her self-centered comment, 'Poor man. I hope they find him, or I'll have to look for another job' distasteful.

Jordan began to think she really was that shallow and brought the coffee time to an end. Easy to do when another busload of tourists pulled up. He made his excuses to Mandy, thanked her for the coffee and said he might be back in the future. He was rewarded with another smile.

On the way back to his car, he called HB. While he waited for the call to pick up, movement near the house caught his eye.

He couldn't be sure, but felt it was Xander Michelson. He looked hell-bent on a mission, and clutched a plastic bag in one hand as he jumped in his car and raced down the drive.

Still watching the fast-disappearing car, he called HB. "I've connected with Mandy Peterson. She's something else alright. Not sure what I got from her is worth much. My sense is she's only as involved as it concerns her own paycheck. Main thing is I've just seen Xander Michelson — well I'm pretty sure it's him — take off. He flew down the driveway like there's no tomorrow."

HB shouted, "What the hell are you wasting time talking with me. Follow him!"

CHAPTER SEVENTEEN

Sunday brunch was in full swing at Maxwell's Bar and Grill. The only day of the week they opened before 11:00. Tables were full and meal orders were flying off the grill. Dorothy had barely greeted Rolin when the rush began. And it was another half hour before she had time to listen to the message HB had left on her phone.

Seizing a lull in orders, she took Rolin to one side. "HB says he's got Jordan following Xander who seemed agitated and in a big hurry to leave the winery. He'll update us as soon as he can. Oh, and I've heard from Shelby. It's about the car."

Before Rolin could respond, a crash came from the kitchen and Dorothy groaned. "I hope those plates were dirty and not an order. I'll go check."

Moments later she returned. "Guess we'll be ordering some new dinnerware. Could have been worse."

Rolin nodded in the direction of the entrance. "And look, the line-up has cleared, so it should start to ease off. Now what were you going to tell me about the car? Etienne Rivard's I assume?"

Dorothy leaned against the bar, her back to the customers. "Yes. Shelby feels whoever grabbed Etienne likely knew his habit of visiting the Mystic District. The police have put in a lot of legwork interviewing store owners and some regular customers. But nothing concrete so far."

She lowered her voice, "You know, the longer this goes on, the more things don't make sense. Shelby has confirmed

Olivia's arrival. She landed at Portland International on the 18th, just as Charlotte told HB. So why let her daughter think she'd only just arrived on the 23rd? Olivia has lied about her arrival and only those closest to Etienne would have known about his regular visits to the Mystic District. The kidnapper has to be close to home. What do you think?"

"Don't forget the kidnapper sent the ransom note, and Etienne's neck chain as proof, directly to Charlotte."

Dorothy hadn't forgotten. Charlotte might not be an adorable toddler to steal heart strings, but she wasn't an adult either. She hadn't deserved to be the recipient of those items, and it made Dorothy angry on her behalf. "That's where I have a problem. Anyone close to the family would know Charlotte – so how mean, insensitive, whatever, is that? But I suppose someone with a focus on hurting the family or looking for cash doesn't really care."

Rolin laid a hand on her arm. "Dee, you and I both know there are no limits to how our fellow humans can act. The trick is not to grow cynical or judge everyone the same way."

She let out a sigh. "I know, but thanks for the reminder. Oh, drink orders coming in, barkeep."

It was midafternoon before they had time to talk again, and this time Rolin had news for her. "You'll never guess who's left a message on my office phone?"

She straightened bottles on a shelf behind the bar and smiled. "C'mon partner. The rush is over. Let's grab a bite to eat and sit for a while, then you can tell me." She moved over to lean into the order area. "Gracie, when those orders are done, can you whip up a couple of omelets for Rolin and me?"

The experienced chef in charge of Sunday brunch had been with the bar and grill since it opened. "Like the kind Max would make for you? Go and sit, I'll bring them over in a minute."

"Perfect. Thanks, Gracie."

The sun had come out in full force, and they chose a spot where they could enjoy its warmth. Dorothy shook her head at Rolin, then grinned at the puzzled look he wore when he asked, "What?"

"I don't know that I've seen you ever look anything but perfect. We've been run off our feet for hours and you still look as if you just showered and dressed. Look at me!" She pointed to evidence of food specks on her blouse and a blob of ketchup on her white sneakers. "Although I do remember one time when you didn't shave for more than a day."

It was a sober memory, reminding Dorothy of the close call she'd had in Detroit. When she'd awoken in her hospital bed, Rolin's unshaven face said he'd never left her side. She pushed it aside. "Sorry, let's not go there right now. Back to what you wanted to say. Who left you a message?"

"Olivia St John-Rivard."

"Really? What did she want?"

Rolin waited while Gracie set their fluffy omelets in front of them.

"She was somewhat vague. Mentioned she was aware I'd done work for her father a few years ago, and hoped she might be able to call on me for legal advice."

"What the heck is her game in all this? Are you going to answer her?"

Rolin finished a mouthful of food. "I would say that depends on you. This can go two ways. If I meet with her and she ends up being a client, anything she says to me I may not be able to share with you. But if I don't meet with her, we could miss out on vital information."

"Don't you just love Catch-22s? Let me think for a bit. One question. If she revealed anything to you of a criminal or life-threatening nature, aren't you able, or even duty-bound, to inform the police?"

"Aha – you do think she's involved, don't you? I would have to tell her that upfront. So, you can see it's not cut and dried. But she can wait for a return call. It is Sunday after all, and my office is closed."

"Women don't generally pull off a kidnapping, but it might explain why Etienne disappeared so easily. She knew he'd be at the Mystic District and surprised him. Maybe she convinced him they needed to go somewhere and talk. They'd come back for his car later. That kind of thing?"

Rolin looked thoughtful but didn't interrupt.

"If she planned all this before she arrived back here, then she's probably been setting this up for a while. Her family is broke and she needs cash. Trying to play the mother card. Or, maybe she's reconciled with Xander, thinking he could solve her money woes. And when she realizes Xander isn't going to be her cash cow — bull? — she goes to plan B which is the kidnap. Sorry, Rolin. I'm kind of thinking out loud."

Rolin sat up straighter. "And if Etienne is killed, Olivia would probably control the purse strings where the winery and her daughter are concerned. I'm going to check into that angle. There should be a will on file, or power of attorney. Charlotte is a minor. And I doubt Etienne would leave that to Xander, despite his godfather status. Etienne knows Xander is hurting financially and an inheritance would be too easy for him to access."

"I guess it wouldn't hurt to follow up with her and see where it leads? I don't expect you to break any confidence, but it could be worthwhile. Especially if you can clarify who controls Michard Estates in the event of Etienne's death. Oh, I hope it doesn't come to that – for Charlotte's sake."

Her phone buzzed with an incoming text from HB. She read it aloud to Rolin.

With Jordan. He followed X to a laundromat downtown. Weird - but we wait.

"A laundromat?" Rolin scratched his head. "This could put a new spin on things."

"Oh, brother," she laughed, as she gathered up their empty plates. "I'd pay to hear you say that in a closing argument."

"For you, a free pass. Anytime."

She smiled but had no time to savor the warmth his comment sparked. Customers waited.

CHAPTER EIGHTEEN

HB joined Jordan in his car. The young investigator was parked a block from the laundromat providing a clear view of the establishment.

"You said he went in 30 minutes ago." HB frowned, "Did he have laundry?

"Well, all he was carrying was his bad mood and a plastic bag. I assume it was laundry. He looked tense and wore the same scowling face as when he left the winery. I don't enjoy doing laundry either, but I hope I never look like that! And yet he drove like a maniac to get here. He would have to make some kind of excuse to the police at the house to leave in such a hurry, I'd think. Doesn't make sense. If he's pissed about doing laundry, why the rush to get here — you can't tell me they don't have a washing machine back at the house. That's his car out front. I wondered if maybe he was late to meet someone."

HB was impressed. Maybe hiring Jordan would work out well. "Good thinking, Jordan. He doesn't know you, so poke your nose into the place and make some excuse about being there if asked."

"Right, I can do that." He had one hand on the door and with the other, passed his camera to HB. "Have a look at the shots I took. The last few will back up what I said about Xander storming off."

Jordan extricated his long lanky frame from the car. He adjusted his reflective sunglasses as he loped off in the direction of the laundromat.

HB put the camera aside; he'd review the photos later. He kept his sights on Jordan through the storefront window and smiled to himself as his protege went through the paces of imitating Columbo, or Jim Rockford. The investigation didn't take long, and he soon returned to the car.

"Learn anything useful?" asked HB as Jordan slid back behind his steering wheel.

"Not much. Other than people can be filthy pigs. You should see some of those machines! No sign of him there now, but I swear he didn't leave. I had my eyes peeled on that entrance the whole time I waited for you. I couldn't have missed him. Honest."

HB reassured Jordan. "Relax, I believe you. I saw you speaking with a couple of customers. They have anything to add?"

"The two women folding clothes? Not much. Said they hadn't seen anyone in the last hour, and what was it to me? I pretended I was looking for a friend." He looked at HB who smirked. "Yeah, I won't make that mistake again. No wonder they brushed me off. But I did notice a door that likely leads to an alley behind the block? Maybe he went through there. What do you think?"

HB mustered a deep sigh. "If his car's still here he must be somewhere in the area. Maybe the alley is a shortcut to ... I don't know. Let's check out the back alley. Drive slow. In case he sees you, I'll crouch down. Don't need to tip our hand he's being tailed."

Jordan followed HB's instructions and they explored the alleyway. Dumpsters and overflowing garbage cans littered the area. They disturbed a couple of hungry cats in search of a meal. No sign of Xander or anyone else.

HB risked sitting up straight as they pulled up to the laundromat's back door. Yes, the door opened next to wooden stairs running up to apartments atop the block of businesses. HB doubted the apartments were featured in any home decor magazine, and probably not up to code.

"I'm not sure he's around here now, Jordan. He'll have to come back for his car, so get yourself ready for surveillance until he reappears. Go back and park, then I'll wait while you grab a sandwich in case you're here for a while."

HB held back a laugh when Jordan reappeared with a bag of sandwiches, snacks and a large coffee. "A word of advice for surveillance. You need to eat and drink, yes, but remember what you take in doesn't stay with you. If you get my drift. You'd best hope Xander reappears before you need the facilities." HB poked at the bulging convenience store bag.

"I didn't think about that. Got it."

HB left Jordan's car but leaned in through the window. "One last thing to keep in mind about Xander Michelson. Did I tell you his boxing nickname? Stonefist Sandy. Just so you know, in case you're ever tempted to get friendly with him." The look on Jordan's face made HB regret, only a little, the teasing. "If you need me, call. And keep me updated if you see him. Right?"

Jordan nodded. "I won't let you down."

***

HB left his young investigator inhaling a sandwich and headed to his own car. Prioritizing things in his mind as always, he called Dorothy.

"Hi, Boss. No joy here at the laundromat so I'm leaving Jordan on surveillance. Xander hasn't yet reappeared. His car's still here - with luck Jordan will spot him when he returns. Ducking into this place might have been a decoy. I don't know, can't get a feel for this yet. Any chance Ted Jellico might have learned anything from Michelson's financials? I'll check with Jake as well."

"I'd say you have things covered there. You sound a little more sure of Jordan now. I'm glad."

"He has potential, but still a little over enthusiastic. Experience will tame that."

"As well you would know. Good point about the financials. I'm meeting with Shelby Keleher in the morning. If I don't get anything from her, I'll check with Ted. I have a feeling she's bound to limit the information she shares with me, and I get it. After Rolin's reveal about the St John's financial downturn, there may be more of a focus on Olivia. I'd say that's one thing she and I share in common. Our suspicions about Charlotte's mother."

"Make that three, Boss. If she has any redeeming qualities, they're buried deep."

"I'll be sure to let Shelby know you're on the same page, too."

HB couldn't identify the reaction he felt when he heard Shelby connected with him in the same sentence. He brushed it off and paid attention to Dorothy who was saying something about dinner.

"Sorry, Boss. Say again."

"I said - there's a roast of beef in the oven. I decided to try my hand at a Sunday dinner and you're more than welcome to join Max, Alanna, and I. Rolin will probably drop by as well. You know how Dad often says cooking a big meal can provide thinking time, helps to settle the monkey brain. Brainstorming might be needed to help find Etienne."

HB waffled. He was tempted, but. "As much as I love a good roast beef dinner, I think I'll say no. Paperwork's piling up and I need to touch base on a couple of other cases."

Dorothy laughed out loud. "I think you're trying to tell me I can't possibly cook like Dad does."

HB relaxed a bit when Dorothy didn't question him on his excuse, and he braved further comment. "Hmm, well seeing as you asked. Can you?"

"Okay, I'll let you off the hook but it's your loss missing out on my superb meal. And I want to hear the minute there's anything to report on Xander."

"As soon as I hear. And, Boss? A roast beef sandwich wouldn't be turned down tomorrow." He imagined her wry smile as he disconnected the call.

***

Jordan was getting antsy, his long legs cramping. A few more basket-laden customers had arrived, but still no Xander, and his car hadn't moved. He cranked up the headbanging playlist on his phone then turned it off. HB would say it was a distraction, and Jordan was determined to not let anything mess this up. He considered walking around the car a couple of times to stretch, but stopped when Xander came out of the laundromat. Not in any rush this time, he sauntered to his car and seemed in no hurry to drive.

He had HB on speed dial. "Shall I follow him or make inquiries inside? He must have come into the premises by the back door."

"Don't follow. I'm halfway to the winery and I'll see if he turns up there. I can't tell you why right now, but I'm sure that's where he'll go. I doubt there'll be anything to learn from inside, but check it out, and then you're free to head home. If there's anything new, call me."

***

What HB didn't share with Jordan was the news he'd just had a call from Charlotte. He'd been on his way back to the *Aye*, when the call came.

"Is this HB?"

"Yeah. Charlotte?" The girl was on the verge of hysterics and HB didn't know how to calm her down over the phone. "Charlotte! Slow down."

"You have to help! Please come!"

"What's happened? Take a breath and then speak. If it helps, I'm heading in your direction right now." He figured she didn't need to know he'd just turned his car around because of her call.

"We've had a call from the kidnapper. They want the money!"

HB's foot pressed harder on the accelerator. "When did the call come? Who spoke?"

"Twenty minutes ago? I answered the phone, but when my mother realized it was from the kidnapper, she pulled the phone away from me. She's useless and all she did was scream and cry. I bet she didn't even get the instructions right! They'll kill my dad!"

HB debated how to treat Charlotte. She wasn't stupid, but he needed her to calm down. What the hell, she probably knew enough from TV anyway. "Charlotte. Think. Did your mother ask for any proof that your dad is still okay?"

"Yes! She did. They wouldn't let me see, but a picture got sent to my mother's cell phone. The kidnapper called on the landline, right? So how does he have my mother's number?"

"Calm down. You're doing fine. I'm almost there. Have more police arrived?"

"Let me check. I'm up in my room to get away from her. Oh, yes, cars are pulling up now. Where are you?"

"Charlotte. Listen to me. I will be there, but I might not be allowed in, understand? The police are in control."

A stronger edge entered Charlotte's voice, replacing the tears. "I'll make sure you get in. No problem. Just get here! Oh, Uncle Xander's here, too. He'll know what to do. He has to get the money!"

CHAPTER NINETEEN

HB pulled in behind the most recent police arrival and parked. Xander's car was visible and had probably arrived about the same time as the cops, as Charlotte said. He shot Dorothy a quick text and then considered how to handle this. Depending on the police presence, he wasn't sure he'd be allowed in. The opportunity handed him by Charlotte to be on the scene was priceless and he didn't want to blow it.

He opened the car door and looked up. Charlotte stood at an upstairs window. She waved and disappeared. He continued on to the front entrance and knocked. As expected, a uniformed office answered the door and HB was ready with an explanation when Charlotte pushed next to the officer. "I want him here. He's my guest."

HB made eye contact with the officer but didn't say a word as he quickly moved past him and followed Charlotte into the house. He passed the room where he'd earlier witnessed the dust-up between Charlotte and her mother. It was well lit against the approaching darkness outside and hummed with activity. Xander held a sobbing Olivia, while a detective and two uniforms hovered nearby.

Charlotte made a tsking sound and kept moving forward. They came into a spacious and modern kitchen. She flipped overhead lighting on. HB didn't care for quartz and granite, too cold for his liking, but he admired the look of the space. Clean and functional, but not institutional. Lights flashed on a dishwasher and a vase of wilting flowers stood guard on a table.

The empty coffee maker caught his attention. "Any chance we could put that to use?"

"What? Oh, coffee? Gross. I'll find the coffee, but you can make it."

He soon had a pot brewing, managing to avoid much small talk until he had a mug in his hand. He tried not to show his surprise when Charlotte cut up a lemon for a tall glass of filtered water. He assumed all kids drank was soda, or worse. Voices could be heard from the other room, but he couldn't make out details.

They sat on bar stools by the kitchen island. Their images were reflected back in the large patio doors. HB disliked the vulnerable feeling he got when windows weren't covered at night. Charlotte tapped black lacquered nails against her water glass. She seemed angrier than upset and HB crossed his fingers she'd stay that way. Easier to deal with anger than tears.

A police officer poked her head into the kitchen. "Everything okay here?"

HB nodded and risked identifying himself as already involved. "Ask Mr. Michelson. I'll stay out of your way though because Charlotte wanted to talk to me."

She left them and HB put his mug down. "Right, Charlotte. Ready to talk about it?"

She lifted her swollen, red-rimmed eyes to look at him. "I'm not a kid, you know. They think they have to protect me or something. When the call came in, they tried to rush me out of the room. But he's my dad and I want him home. I didn't leave the room."

"Can you remember exactly what the caller said?"

"I'll never forget. The voice was all weird though. Made me think of Darth Vader. *I said no police. So now time's up. 450 thousand or he dies.* When I told him I wanted to speak to my dad, she grabbed the phone and started screaming at him. And then the cop started to coach her and got her to ask for proof he's still alive. I could have done that!"

"Great detail about the voice, Charlotte. You said the kidnapper sent a picture as proof?"

"I didn't get to see it, but I think it was a picture of Dad holding a copy of today's newspaper."

HB nodded. "Makes sense. Whoever the kidnapper is, he's not stupid. But how did he have your mother's cell number. Did you hear her give it to him?"

"Maybe," she whispered. "I don't know for sure. She could have when they pushed me away. Sorry."

HB patted her hand. "You're doing great. How about we sit here nice and quiet?"

The hint of a smile brightened her face. "So we can listen in?"

HB held out a knuckled fist, which Charlotte bumped in kind. The conspirators sat in silence and listened as voices fraught with tension volleyed back and forth in the next room.

HB wondered if tough guy Stonefist Sandy was going to cry as he berated Olivia. He apparently didn't care personal information was being thrown out for all to hear. "Why didn't you tell me your family's broke! They would have paid the ransom, for Charlotte's sake. How could you not tell me!"

Olivia's response was muffled by her tears, but HB wondered how real her distress was. Judging by the tightened lips on his companion, Charlotte probably wasn't impressed either. With little to no commentary from the police, HB figured they might be wondering the same thing.

Olivia's voice grew stronger. "Stop whining Xander and concentrate! We have to find the money somehow. Listen. Before you were — let go — did Etienne still have a safe in his office? He was always so proud of the fact he kept cash on hand, not just in the house safe, but out in his office. Maybe?"

The detective spoke. "Either of you have the combinations for these safes?"

Dead silence and HB imagined the looks passing between Olivia and Xander. If they'd known the combinations at one time, surely Etienne would have changed them once the pair were no longer on the scene. He looked at Charlotte and raised an eyebrow.

"I bet I know what it is," she said.

HB grinned. "I think the police will want to listen to you now. C'mon."

He grabbed her hand and they rushed into the living room. Olivia glowered at her. "You need to let us handle this, Charlotte."

Charlotte ignored her and went straight to the detective. "I might know the combination. It will be the same for both."

Xander made a move to hug her, and HB was surprised to see her pull back. Maybe she was growing up fast and that meant reassessing the adults in her life. He'd have to ask her about her reaction later. Right now, she had the room's attention.

"Speak up Charlotte. We're waiting!" Olivia's tears had dried up, her expression begging her daughter to reveal the information.

Charlotte ignored her and spoke to the detective. "I don't know your name."

HB had never met him either and waited for him to respond. If the detective, well dressed and about HB's age, was smart, he wouldn't patronize Charlotte. HB kept his fingers crossed.

"Charlotte, I'm Jeremiah Gladstone. What can you tell us about the combinations?"

No one spoke. HB found himself holding his breath until she asked, "Do you have a piece of paper?"

Gladstone tore a page out of his notebook and handed over his pen. She wrote and handed it back. "This is only for the police, okay?"

"If that's what you want, Charlotte."

HB dared a glance at Olivia. The blotches of red on her face spoke volumes. Charlotte ignored her, and Xander.

"Yes, that's what I want. And I will show you where the safes are. Not them. And HB? Thank you for listening."

Xander and Olivia moved to follow after Charlotte and the detective, but one of the uniformed officers stopped them. HB couldn't read the emotion on Xander's face, but he wasn't a happy camper. Betrayal never added to anyone's good looks.

He hung back to one side, observing. Neither Olivia nor Xander spoke to each other. He assumed they didn't want to speak in front of witnesses, but body language? Xander paced and didn't offer any sympathetic vibes to his former lover. Or were they still former? Had something changed; was that what set Charlotte off? Olivia threw herself into a wingback chair and drummed her fingers on the armrest.

A door closed and Xander moved to the front window. "They're heading to the office. And Gladstone's got a package in one hand."

"Are you speaking to me now?" Olivia's voice would freeze alcohol.

Xander turned back from the window and noticed HB as if for the first time. His fists clenched and HB tensed as Xander came to within inches of HB's face. "I don't know what the hell you're playing at, but you're not family. I'll be talking to Charlotte. She doesn't need to deal with you."

HB didn't flinch and held Xander's stare until the man finally looked away. The uniform in the room had also gone on alert, but HB waved him off. "It's okay. This is a hard time for everyone."

He wanted to ask if details had been given as to the ransom drop off, but his presence there stood on thin ice, and it was better not to ask. Could there possibly be enough money on hand to satisfy the kidnapper? The amount was off as well. 450 thousand. Why not an even 500? Something tugged at HB's memory, but it would have to wait.

Silence gained the upper hand and a wall clock's ticking marked the passing of minutes while they waited for the others to return. HB took out his phone and texted Dorothy. It would be late before things wrapped up here, and Dorothy said she planned to meet with Shelby Keleher first thing in the morning. Her last text came with instructions. I think you should be there too. HB agreed.

A door opened and rushing footsteps announced the return of Charlotte and the detective. She ran into the room ahead of the detective. "We've got the money! Almost all of it!"

Olivia exhaled. "Oh, thank God. But not enough? How much do we need?"

The detective laid a hand on Charlotte's shoulder. "Please. Let me. You need to catch your breath."

She nodded and moved closer to HB and let Gladstone talk. "I've done a rough count. There's $435,000 here."

"It will have to do!" Olivia's high-pitched plea pierced HB's skull.

"He'll have to understand. Won't he?" Xander's question couldn't be answered.

"Ouch!" Olivia wailed and collapsed back into the chair, clutching at her stomach.

"Ma'am? What's wrong?" Detective Gladstone brushed Xander aside and stood over her.

"It's my ulcer. I ran out of medication, and of course with all of this, it's flared up." She winced in pain and then looked at Xander. "Can you go into town and get what I need?"

"Ma'am. I can send an officer."

"No but thank you. Xander knows what I need. And to be honest, I need him out of here right now. I'm feeling overwhelmed and claustrophobic or something. Just go, Xander. Go!"

Gladstone nodded at him. "Go but be quick about it."

Xander looked at his watch. "I hope there's a drugstore open this time of night. And on a Sunday."

"Dammit it, Xander. Figure it out! Don't be useless for once in your life."

HB thought the relationship threads around him were unravelling faster than an old sweater. It was time for him to go, too.

He pulled Charlotte aside. "You may have saved the day, knowing the combination."

She grinned. "Easy. My birthdate, duh!"

"Well, still. It was up to you. And now I need to go. Will be you okay? Gladstone seems to get you, so talk to him. Got it?"

With no warning, Charlotte flung her arms about him and squeezed. "You're the best and really helped me today. I'll be okay, now."

He disentangled himself and tried to find his voice. "Part of my job, that's all."

And then he made his escape back to his car. He'd need more than one beer to put this day behind him.

CHAPTER TWENTY

Driving to the police department to meet Dorothy and Shelby Keleher, HB wondered if he should talk with Max about Charlotte. He was out of his depth dealing with kids in the first place and Charlotte had him confused. Last thing he needed was some teenage girl thinking the wrong things about him. There was no one he'd feel comfortable discussing this with, but at least Max had had experience raising a daughter.

He pulled into a visitor's spot, noting Dorothy's Jeep a few spaces away. A text first thing from her earlier told him there was a development she'd share at the meeting. He doubted it was good news or she would have called with details.

The morning sun glinted off his side mirror. He'd need his sunglasses later. His unsettled mood he credited to concerns over Charlotte, but why did he grow more antsy the closer he got to his destination?

Dispensing brief nods of greeting, he walked closer to Keleher's desk. She and Dorothy were deep in conversation. Dorothy must have brought the coffees in with her. A third cup, unopened, awaited him. They hadn't spotted him yet and HB had a brief, illuminating, moment to connect his uneasiness with Keleher. No, he corrected himself, it's not uneasiness, but an unfamiliar spark of excitement. He wanted to see the Sergeant. And then Keleher glanced his way. He met her eyes and quickly found something else to look at. "Boss. Sorry I'm late. What a day yesterday, eh?"

"And another day we're no closer to finding Etienne Rivard." Dorothy's sigh of frustration matched HB's take on the case as well. Dorothy tapped the chair next to her for him to sit.

"Boss, you said there was a development. Anything helpful?" HB turned to the Sergeant. "Dorothy has my breakdown on events yesterday, so I'm sure you're up to speed, Sergeant."

Shelby kept her eyes on HB, offering a rare smile. "Yes, HB, thank you." Her eyes still held his, but there was a wall. HB didn't return the smile, unsure of the territory he was in. The smile slipped away. "Apologies. Would you prefer I call you Mr. Bartholomew?"

"HB's fine," he managed to mumble, uncomfortable — or encouraged — with the tone of familiarity. He didn't miss the twinkle of amusement in Dorothy's eyes, causing his inner turmoil to rise. As if dealing with Charlotte wasn't bad enough, now he had to decipher signals from Shelby Keleher, although it wasn't necessarily a bad thing.

Keleher took command. "The development, yes. Details, finally, for a ransom drop."

HB tensed. "When? Nothing had come in while I was there. It must have happened after I left?"

Keleher nodded. "9:13 p.m. to be exact. Olivia St John-Rivard answered it. She was told to drop the money at 6:00 p.m. today." Keleher emptied her coffee cup and tossed it into a bin beside her desk.

"Where?" HB never cared for delaying tactics and Keleher seemed to enjoy dragging out the details.

She pushed a piece of paper toward him, with an address. "Recognize this?"

No way. The laundromat Jordan had tailed Xander to. "What the ...?"

Dorothy added. "Oh, it gets better. The demand is for the money to be put into a pillowcase and placed into a specific dryer marked 'Out of Order'."

"So Xander has to be involved, doesn't he? This is not a freaking coincidence. I knew there was something about him I didn't like." He drank from his coffee and let his thoughts connect. "Oh, hell."

"What is it?" asked Dorothy.

"Well, it's Charlotte, of course. Her father's missing, could be dead. Her mother, useless, and the only other adult she had in her life is Xander." HB's memories of his own teenage years and the challenges he had faced, surfaced. "She's just a kid. We have to find her father."

He pointed to paperwork on Keleher's desk. "So where do we stand?"

"Just before you arrived, HB, we were talking about the Rivard family dynamics."

"Yes," said Keleher, "and HB I'd be interested in your impressions of the Rivard family. You've dealt with all of them by now. The ex, the daughter Charlotte. And what do you make of the uncle and former business partner, Xander Michelson?"

"You're picking him up, right? Or at least tailing him?"

"We do know what we're doing, HB. Trust me, we're on it."

Right, he'd heard that before. The room had closed in on him and the sooner he could finish here and get back on this case, the better. If Dorothy hadn't been there, he might not have held his temper. For now, he'd play nice with the cops.

"The St John-Rivards. Lots going on there, most under the surface I'd say. Olivia is probably still a gold-digger. Concerned with her own self. Daughter comes second, and she knows it. No wonder Charlotte has no time for her own mother. And she seems to be disenchanted with her uncle right now as well. Kid's smart, she probably smells a rat, too. I'm pretty sure any tears Olivia might shed over Etienne are either a display, or concern for her own status. For better or worse, Charlotte seems to think I'm her friend. Which has proved useful, and I will do my best to keep the connection." This was better, HB was back on familiar ground, and focused on what he knew. Dorothy's nod let him know this was his show. Don't hold anything back. Which meant these two strong, and smart, women were trying to work together.

Dorothy laughed. "Oh, HB. I knew you could be a father figure after all."

HB shrugged. "Not funny, Boss."

Keleher broke in. "And Xander Michelson? Dorothy says you and a colleague had him under surveillance yesterday. But I'd like to hear it in your own words."

He proceeded to tell her about the surveillance of Xander and the laundromat. The same laundromat where the ransom was to be dropped? He regretted dismissing Jordan from the location. Bad mistake on his part and he only hoped it wouldn't come back to bite him.

"At this point I'd say the surveillance turned up empty with nothing to report. I left Jordan there for a while and was on my way home when Charlotte called me. She was upset and I decided to return to the winery. On the way, Jordan called to say Michelson had left the laundromat. I told him I was headed to the estate, and he could call it quits on the surveillance."

"As usual, HB, your timing is impeccable."

"Thanks, Boss. Anyway, Charlotte saved the day by knowing the combination of the safes. You're probably aware they almost have the full amount of the requested ransom." HB snapped his fingers. "Boss, I forgot. The ransom amount requested was $450,000. Coincidence or not, that's the same amount of money Michelson lost when Rivard bankrupted him."

Dorothy turned to Keleher. "Have your team confirmed this same amount?"

"Yes. And I don't believe in coincidences. But back to why you followed Xander to the laundromat in the first place?"

"My investigator, Jordan Klein, noticed him leave the winery. Because he seemed agitated, I advised Jordan to follow him. Which he did - to the laundromat. I joined him there a few minutes later. We were looking into details about the laundromat to see if there's a connection, and obviously there is."

Keleher wanted more from HB. "And what did you learn from Michelson about his behavior?"

"I didn't get a chance to question him. In hindsight I can see the pieces falling into place. I should have clued in sooner!"

"Chill, HB. Anyone would have done the same. Tell the sergeant, in your own words, what happened after you arrived back at the estate?"

"Charlotte was waiting for me and met me at the door, bypassing her mother and Michelson. The situation at the winery is tense to say the least. Charlotte has more brains than Olivia and Xander put together. She's my point of reference with that household. Olivia is out of control, treating Xander like an errand boy, and like I said, by the time I'd left, Xander was off Charlotte's Christmas list."

HB watched Keleher lean back in her chair. There was no warmth in her face as she tipped her head slightly back. Thinking mode?

Coming back to attention, her voice was clipped and dismissive. "The personalities involved in this case are complicated on different levels. Thank you both for your input. We'll be in touch."

Dorothy stood and said, "I do hope you can understand we only want to help in this situation. Xander Michelson is still my client and he, along with the others in the family, are our priority. However, in light of this development, he will be handled with utmost caution. At this point he must suspect we could be on to him. But anything we learn we'll pass on to you."

"Likewise, Dorothy. I'm not used to working with outside help, but I can see the benefits. HB, you appear to have a good connection with the daughter. Do what you can to ensure that line of communication stays open - it may prove valuable."

HB mumbled his thanks. The door opened to an officer from the squad room.

"Sarge, we've had a call from the winery. Gladstone is saying the young girl, Charlotte, has gone from the house. She left a note to say she's looking for her dad as no one else is doing anything."

HB jumped to his feet, ready to pace. "Damn it anyway. Why couldn't she stay put?"

Shelby answered the constable. "Thank you, Wyatt, meeting in five minutes." She stood up and was all business. "If you hear from Charlotte, we need to know, understood? Now if you'll excuse me ... We have a lot of money to keep an eye on."

"We'll get out of your way, of course," said Dorothy. The look she gave to HB told him to keep his concerns to himself.

Neither spoke until they reached the parking lot and stopped at HB's car.

"Boss, I'd like to start looking for Charlotte. She's too young to be out on the streets searching for her dad."

"Keep me posted HB. I'm heading back to the Grill. Lunchtime rush and Rolin's busy with clients."

They parted company, heading in different directions. She returned to Max's and HB drove to the winery. He wanted to talk with Olivia and Xander before heading off to look for Charlotte. He hoped her drama-queen mother could give him an idea where Charlotte might go.

***

No shortage of police presence today, but HB had no problem entering the house this time. Newbie Detective Gladstone greeted him and pulled him aside. "HB, isn't it? My boss has issued us a directive, and you have clearance to speak to whomever you like. She assures me you're on the level."

"I am. But Detective, how did Charlotte leave with no one noticing? She can't drive, so did she walk, or did someone pick her up? You were supposed to be keeping an eye on these people."

Gladstone held up a hand. "Hang on. I've just come on duty. She was already gone before I arrived this morning. You know what teenagers are like."

"Actually, I don't, teenagers or children of any age. I understand she left a note - can I see it?" HB bordered on being pissed at the girl, just after he'd all but boasted he had a connection with her. He thought they'd been on the same page.

"Yes, sure. I can tell you that no one on duty saw her leave. We don't even have a timeline of her departure. She was seen hanging around in the barrel room late last night. When questioned she said she couldn't sleep. Her note was found on Mandy Peterson's desk."

"So, no one knows when she left the barrel room. Did she come back to the house or leave straight from there. Is her phone being tracked? Was she seen talking on her phone, did a friend pick her up? How does a fourteen-year-old get around without transportation?"

HB understood eyes couldn't be everywhere, but he was more than disappointed that Charlotte had pulled a fast one. Blame shifting on Gladstone's part didn't help, but berating the detective would only be counterproductive.

"Obviously, we messed up here. The assumption was she returned to her room, but the Peterson girl found her note when she started work this morning."

Assumption! HB bit down on a retort and kept his tone even. "You know what they say when you assume. Where do we go from here, then. Where is her mother? Does she have any idea where Charlotte might be?"

"She's been in her room since returning from the ransom drop-off. She was upset. I was about to speak with her when you arrived."

HB forced himself to take a deep breath before he spoke again. Charlotte had got under his skin and now he was worried about her. Losing his cool with Gladstone wouldn't help matters.

"After you've spoken to her, please tell Ms. St John-Rivard I'm here and need to speak to her about Charlotte. That should be just as upsetting as dropping off the ransom, don't you think? And Michelson - where is he?"

"You just missed Mr. Michelson. He left when I told him Charlotte had gone."

HB fought the urge to pace, his automatic response to being stressed. He needed to keep a clear head. "What are you waiting for? Go find the mother!"

Under his breath he muttered. "I need a coffee."

"Oh, I can show you where the kitchen is." Gladstone had turned back.

"I know where the kitchen is. I'll be waiting for Olivia St. John-Rivard in there. One more thing. Did Michelson bring back the medication she wanted last night?"

"I'll have to check."

"Do that. Oh, and after you've found those two, I want a word with Mandy Peterson, in here, too."

HB poured a coffee and took out his notebook. He really needed to know what time Michelson had returned with the medication.

CHAPTER TWENTY-ONE

Dorothy parked in her reserved spot beside Maxwell's and hurried inside to help with lunchtime customers. Most days she could resist the mouthwatering dishes coming from the kitchen, but today hunger pangs rumbled. She checked her watch. It was nearly one o'clock. If Rolin emerged from his office ...

"Speak of the devil." She teased as Rolin joined her behind the bar.

"I hope that's not a bad thing, Dee?"

"That would be telling, wouldn't it?" she laughed, handing him a towel. "Help me with these glasses and then I have a suggestion."

Her suggestion was one Rolin readily agreed to, and forty minutes later found them at a roadside diner ready to order a late lunch. They sat at a table, bypassing most of the booths. Those cushioned seats had seen better days.

"Eating at Maxwell's is like a busman's holiday. This makes a nice change. Good call, Dee."

"I'm happy you approve. I can't believe how hungry I am, and I think the house burger has my name on it." She laid the menu down. "We've both had a busy morning, I think. I spent about an hour with Shelby. This case just doesn't want to quit! And how about you? Any interesting clients today?"

As they started their meal, Rolin gave an overview of his morning, but kept it brief. "As you can see, nothing exciting. I'm more interested to know what's happening with you. Did the information about the downturn in the St John finances have any bearing?"

"Yes, thank you. It did. What you were able to forward from Anjali was more in depth than the police discovered. I have a feeling someone in the department there wasn't pleased to come up short."

"And while we're on the subject of all things related to Olivia St John Rivard," said Rolin, "I have spoken to her and diplomatically explained it would be a conflict of interest for me to be involved in any legal issues with her. I don't need her kind of aggravation. If I'm going to work for financially strapped clients, I prefer the local clientele."

"And how did she take the turn-down, because I'm sure she took it personally."

"Let's just say I didn't offer any referrals because I'd like to keep my friends. Shakespeare understood what a shrew is and now I think I do as well."

Dorothy laughed. "On that subject, we can both agree. HB seems to know how to deal with her. Although if push came to shove, I'd enjoy a verbal sparring match with her."

Rolin signaled the server for another beer. Dorothy passed on more wine. "I'm the one driving."

"Correct me if I'm wrong, but I'd say you're enjoying working with HB on this case. Maybe you pulled back from investigations too soon?"

She popped the last French fry into her mouth, considering Rolin's observation. "I'm torn, you know? I feel quite content working behind the bar and running Maxwell's with you. But there are times ..."

"When you miss the action?"

She nodded. "Time will tell. In the meantime, I'm happy with how HB is handling things. Oh, I didn't tell you."

"Tell me what?"

"I think there might be a spark of some sort between HB and Shelby. Anytime I've seen the two of them together, they seem to do a kind of awkward dance around each other. HB often looks like a fish out of water. Or maybe it's dealing with Charlotte that has him kerfuffled."

"Ah, women troubles. HB is more comfortable dealing with criminals than a romantic interest, I'm sure. Do you know Shelby well enough yet to test the waters around her?"

"Oh, no. I'm steering clear for now. They're both grownups as far as I can tell."

The server appeared and removed their empty plates. Dorothy sat forward, resting her chin in one hand. "My competitive side wants to find out what this laundromat connection is before the police do, but it might risk the truce I have with Shelby right now. I'm just thinking of future alliances, in the event Reg Pierson takes a permanent leave. He and I had a good rapport, but it's not so easy with Shelby."

"Need the wisdom of Solomon, is that what you're saying?" Rolin's way of understanding was one of the things she loved best about him. "Why don't you, and HB, continue with your investigations and see what turns up. If you get there before the police, I know you have the knack to make a suggestion to steer Keleher in the right direction."

Dorothy laid her hand atop Rolin's, then pulled away and leaned back in her chair. "I knew you'd help me see it better." She reached for her wallet. "And this is on me today. It was my suggestion after all."

Rolin put his hands up. "I wasn't even going to try."

"You're learning. C'mon. Nice as this is, we need to get back. And I'm waiting to hear from HB after his session with Olivia. I know he'd rather be out looking for Charlotte, but questioning Olivia has to come first. I have a feeling she knows a lot more than she lets on."

***

HB couldn't relax while he waited on Olivia or Mandy to join him. Good thing the kitchen was spacious – it gave him pacing room. He checked his phone, again, on the off chance there was a message from Charlotte. Where the hell had she gone? He'd already left two voice mails and sent three texts, any more would be redundant.

He moved to the patio doors and looked out at the acres of vines stretching before him. It was a great view, but he preferred the water. When this case was over, he resolved to hook up with Max for an overdue day of fishing.

A wave of Olivia's perfume announced her arrival before he could turn around.

"I was told you wanted to see me, so here I am. I don't have much time and need to get downtown shortly."

The concern for her daughter was underwhelming, but he wasn't going to touch that for now. "Yes, thank you. Just a couple of questions. About the latest ransom demand. What time did the call come in?"

"I think it was just after nine." She inhaled deeply and HB wondered if more tears were in the offing. But no, the oxygen was fuel for anger. She moved closer to him, and he allowed a small flinch. He figured she'd expect that, but he was wise to her intimidation tactics. She seemed satisfied at his reaction and backed away. "You and the police are doing nothing – nothing – to find my husband."

"Your ex-husband."

She glared at him but didn't respond.

HB calmly moved to the kitchen counter where his notebook lay and flicked it open to the page he wanted. "And what time did Mr. Michelson leave, at your request, for a drugstore run?"

"The police were here, they know." Her eyes flashed. "And you were still here as well. Pretending to be important. You heard me tell him to leave, so why are you asking? Don't you people know how to take notes or something?"

Trying to undermine him was a tactic others had tried in the past and failed. "Yes, but I'd also like to hear it from you to ensure the information lines up ... with my notes. And, I should inform you that Quail Investigations has the full authority of the police department to ask you, or anyone else, whatever questions we feel would be helpful."

He thought he'd judged right; she was about to claim he had no business asking her questions. If she was angry at his right to be there, she hid it from him. She had more faces than a deck of Queens, but he was beginning to recognize her swings.

"Fine. Xander left here a bit before nine. He was worried the drug store would be closed, but I know they're open till ten. He had lots of time. In fact, he was back before ten, with what I needed. You left just after he did." Her voice grew cold. "And just what did my daughter have to say to you? Is that why she's not here?"

HB was momentarily caught off guard, but let it play out. "When Charlotte comes home, I suggest you ask her yourself. I have no idea why she's not here. Do you?"

Olivia sniffed. "You are aware we don't have a very good relationship right now, aren't you? So don't even bother asking if I know who her friends are, or where she might have gone. Her father would know all that, but of course, he's not here, is he!"

She fumbled in an oversized red purse and handed him a photo of Charlotte. "Before you ask, here is a picture of my daughter. It's taken a while ago, but it might help."

He reached for the photo and took his own picture of it with his phone. This would have to go straight to the cops for distribution.

HB stood, unmoved by the fresh torrent of crocodile tears. He briefly wondered if she'd ever been on the stage. Movement in the hallway near the kitchen stopped further speculation. Mandy Peterson stood there, with Detective Gladstone. HB nodded at them. "Give us one minute, okay?"

He turned back to Olivia, who dabbed at her nose and eyes with a sodden tissue. "Thank you for your time and the photo. We are doing everything we can to find Mr. Rivard. If you hear from Charlotte, please have her call the police or me. I won't hold you up any longer so you can get to your appointment." If she told him she was getting her hair done, or one of those spa things, he'd lose it on her. "Oh, and exactly where is your appointment?"

"Not that it's any of your business, but I have a meeting at a local bank." She rattled off the address, and thankfully left without another word, but managed to jostle Mandy Peterson on the way out.

He handed over the picture of Charlotte to Gladstone. "From her mother."

"Thanks, I was about to ask if she had one. The sooner we can circulate it the better."

HB turned to face the receptionist. "Hi, Mandy, I won't keep you long." He made note of Olivia's bank address, which he would get confirmed shortly.

"Is she okay?" Mandy turned to view Olivia's retreating back.

"Upset over the situation, as I'm sure you can appreciate. Now, I only wanted to ask you about the note Charlotte left. You didn't see her, or talk with her?"

This was another woman HB suspected of changing moods to suit the situation and by now he had no time for phony responses. Maybe she read something in his face because she came across as genuine, for a change.

"No, sorry. Like I told the cops, I found it on my desk when I arrived this morning. I've only ever spoken to her a couple of times – she's kind of a moody kid you know? So, I really don't know why she chose me to leave it with." She stopped for a breath, and then asked, "No word then on Etienne? Do you think he'll be found? It's been so long ..."

HB shook his head. "We are still looking. Now, the note please. Can I see it?"

She handed over a piece of paper. "Sorry, cops have the original — 'just in case', they said."

You can tell the police, or Mr. HB, but NOT my mother. I've gone to look for my dad. Nobody else is looking for him!

Damn, not a clue as to where, or how, she was going to start looking.

Mandy twisted the steel post above her eyebrow. "Um, for what it's worth. If I were Charlotte and didn't want to get found out, I'd have left when everyone was asleep. She used to have a bicycle behind one of the buildings. I always told her it should be locked up because it's not a cheap one. Anyway, I checked on my way over here and it's gone."

"Thanks, Mandy, that's a start."

"I hope she is the one who finds Etienne. Piss on the cops anyway – no offense to you."

"None taken. Quick question. Is Xander Michelson in the office with you today?"

"He was there when I arrived. I don't think he noticed the note on my desk, but I showed it to him right away and he took off. Never said a word but didn't look so good."

"Good to know, thanks. Is he managing to focus on winery business with all this going on? And now I imagine he's worried about Charlotte."

She shrugged. "Who knows. Not like we're good friends or anything. Besides he shoves most of the work stuff off on Tom Romano."

"If you think of anything that might help us find Charlotte, you can text me," he handed her a business card, "or talk to any of the police hanging around."

"Sure. Can I go now?"

She left, and HB put his empty coffee mug in the dishwasher. He turned to see Gladstone standing behind him. "Thought you'd want to know. Techs have determined

Charlotte turned off her phone pretty much as soon as she left here. There have been no signals since 1:30 a.m. this morning."

"Mandy was right then; she did leave in the small hours. She thinks she may have taken a bicycle. You let your Sergeant know and I'll tell my boss."

He got into his car and called Dorothy.

"Olivia St John-Rivard has a personality for every occasion. Not sure she knows what the word sincere means. I determined the ransom call came in after Michelson left for the drugstore and before he returned, with the requested medicine. And now I've learned Charlotte likely left here around 1:30 in the morning, on a bike. She won't know, then, that the ransom money has been paid. She's probably headed downtown and knows about the Mystic District. It's about a twenty-five-minute bike ride from here. I'm going to start there."

"Thanks for the update, Number One. I'll be here all day unless you need me, so keep in touch. Oh, and what about Xander Michelson?"

"Found out about the note from Charlotte and took off. Far as I know hasn't been heard from since."

CHAPTER TWENTY-TWO

HB left the winery and drove with purpose toward the Mystic District. He'd learned Etienne sometimes frequented there with Charlotte in tow. Opening the car window allowed fresh air to flow over him in hopes of obliterating the overpowering remnants of Olivia's perfume. His lack of experience with teenagers had him at a loss to make sense of Charlotte's actions. And then there was Mandy. Older than Charlotte, but in need of even more growing up. He grudgingly gave her points for noticing Charlotte's bike was missing.

Glancing at the sky he noted clouds gathering and predicted rain before too long. Traffic was heavier than usual for this time of day, and he fumed as a car stalled in front of him. The delay forced him to slow down and think.

His thoughts rippled in multiple directions, but at the center was Charlotte. At her age, she lacked street skills and would be easy prey for any number of low life scum prowling the streets. He couldn't help but snicker when he recalled her knowledge of police tactics gained from too much TV. It might give her an edge. That made him think of Shelby Keleher. Damn - why did she keep intruding when he was concentrating on Charlotte?

An opportunity to move around the stalled car arose and he shook off those thoughts as he accelerated. He needed to focus on Charlotte. Where would a young girl like her likely go?

He parked a block away from the edges of Portland's Mystic District. He preferred the city's image of craft breweries, but knew this area promoted crystals, spiritual shops and occult stuff. Right up Charlotte's alley. His only interest in the area would be the popular coffee shops. He had no time alternative mystic mumbo-jumbo. He flashed his phone with Charlotte's image everywhere he went. "Are you sure you haven't seen her in your store? The police will be asking as well."

HB repeated his plea in six stores, with negative results. One woman offered to use her Tarot cards and another her physic powers to find the missing girl.

"Er, thanks, but no thanks. I'll keep looking. Please, if you see her call the police, or me," he said handing out his card.

At the end of the street, after stopping window-shoppers to look at Charlotte's picture he decided it was time he touched base with Dorothy. He could do with a caffeine hit as well and stopped at the next establishment.

He cradled the phone against his ear as he popped open the lid on a steaming americano. "Boss, I'm getting nowhere. I've seen a few of the cops from the precinct asking around as well. There's no joy here. I'm heading back to the laundromat." He glanced at his watch, almost five p.m. "The drop is scheduled for six, so I'd like to be nearby. Yes, I'll keep a low profile. Think I'll get Jordan back on this as well. Xander wouldn't recognize him."

"Stay on it HB. We're no closer to connecting Xander to this, but I never underestimate my instincts. So be on guard. We've seen his temper."

"Instincts, red flags. Whatever. I'd say there's more than a connection, but I can't be seen tripping over the cops."

"You won't, HB. You're good at what you do. Listen, I had a thought. If Charlotte's been gone, what, more than twelve hours now? She's probably hungry, so check the fast-food places. The weather could get her off the streets as well."

"Speaking from experience on teenage appetites?" He scoffed, not expecting her to respond. "If Xander doesn't show at the laundromat, I'll swing by the gym to see if he's been there today. But my priority is Charlotte. She's hell bent on finding her father."

Just then the skies opened, releasing the rain in torrents. "Gotta go, Boss. I need to find this girl before she gets soaked if she's not sheltering somewhere."

He ran back towards his car, grateful for his waterproof jacket and ball cap. Wiping the rain from his face he turned his car and headed a few blocks toward the laundromat where Jordan had previously seen Xander.

Rivulets of rain pulsed down HB's car windows as he parked. The storm had darkened the day, and fluorescent lighting inside the laundry facility revealed only one person. Not Xander. HB drummed his fingers on the steering wheel. "C'mon Jordan, where are you?" He hoped the rain would distract any cops on surveillance from noticing him. They weren't easy to spot, but had to be nearby, waiting for the ransom drop to be picked up.

Ten minutes later, Jordan finally arrived. He ran from his car to HB's, but still managed to bring the rain inside with him, sprinkling drops over the dashboard and seat.

HB brought him up to date on Charlotte's disappearance and growing suspicions Xander was involved. He stressed the urgency to find her. "If Michelson is involved, the family ties won't matter - Charlotte needs to stay far away from him."

"What does this girl look like? I didn't see her at the house."

"Check your phone. I sent her photo a few minutes ago. She's only 14 but trying for older. She's sporting the dark and angry look, long braided hair, with some blue or purple mixed in, and jet-black nails."

Jordan looked amused but kept to the job at hand. "Understood. So, what's the plan?"

"Check out the laundromat for any signs of Xander, back door, washroom, maybe there's a storeroom. But don't, and I mean do not, pay any attention to the dryer marked out of order."

"Right, lots of other eyes are watching it. Got it. And if there's no sign of Xander?"

"Leave by the back door. Alleys run all the way up to the Mystic District. Head in that direction. I suspect Charlotte may have gone there. Act casual, police will be back there as well. If you get stopped, then you'll have to own up."

"Other than Xander, what should I be looking for?"

HB sucked air through his teeth in frustration. "Signs of Charlotte, man!"

"Of course, sorry. Stupid of me."

"Forget it. We're all under stress and a deadline. Now go and stay in touch."

Jordan left HB's car and hurried to the entrance. It was teeming and difficult to see into the laundry facility. HB peered through his windshield and barely made out Jordan before he disappeared from view. Now he had to wait.

Waiting was necessary, but also a waste of time. He had to trust Jordan to be his eyes because he sure as hell would rather be checking out the alleyways than stuck in his car. He resisted checking his watch, and hoped the cops were better positioned to move when the ransom was picked up. Assuming it got picked up. He knew the best laid plans ...

His phone buzzed. Jordan. "What've you got?"

"HB," Jordan's voice had risen with excitement. "I'm about two blocks away from you. In the alley like you said. There's a bike, an expensive one. Looks like it was thrown toward a dumpster but missed. And a backpack covered in goth symbols, and the initials CR on one of the straps. I haven't touched anything."

Adrenaline flooded over HB. Charlotte's things, his gut told him. "Great work. I'll be right ... Hang on, I have another call."

"HB – help!"

His stomach shriveled at the fear he heard. "Charlotte? Where are you? Are you okay?"

"On 23rd I think. My phone's nearly dead. Please hurry."

He recognized the desperation in her voice and had to find her fast. "Is there a store or building nearby you can go into?"

She choked back a sob. "I see a bookstore? Should I go there? I lost a shoe. They won't let me in."

A warning beep from her phone told HB he had to move. "Go there. I'll find you."

"I knew you would. He nearly ..." The line went dead.

He reconnected with Jordan. "You stay there. I've heard from Charlotte. Tell the police what you've found and that I'll call when I've got her safe." He didn't wait for an answer but gunned his car out into traffic in a race against time to find Charlotte.

CHAPTER TWENTY-THREE

Dorothy couldn't concentrate – shifting her focus from the pouring rain to anxiously wondering what was happening with HB. Had he found Charlotte yet? Mondays were generally the quietest day of the week and not for the first time did she wonder about closing Maxwell's permanently on Mondays. Shifting to a 6-day week would free up time to spend with her father. And Rolin. She smiled to herself. Ever since his friend Anjali had surfaced, she found she'd been thinking of Rolin anytime they weren't working together.

She tore her gaze away from the rain spattered windows. Another check of her phone confirmed no new updates from HB. She berated herself for not being more in tune regarding Xander Michelson at their first meeting. Seriously, who reports a crime before it's happened? She should have known then something was off about him.

Water under the bridge now.

"Penny for your thoughts?"

She turned and smiled at Rolin, who had come up behind her with clean cutlery for the tables she'd been wiping down.

"Missing out on the action, I think. The ransom drop is any minute and HB, with Jordan, are trying to find Charlotte. I don't have a good feeling about any of this."

"And no news from Sergeant Keleher either, then?"

Dorothy shook her head. "No. Waiting truly is one of the hardest things to do." She looked around the room which only had three tables occupied. "I've been doing some thinking. Let's get back behind the bar where it's easier to talk."

Talking over her idea of having Maxwell's closed on Mondays with Rolin provided the distraction she needed. To her surprise, he was more than agreeable. "I agree, Dee. Mondays are the least busy days. Rarely is anyone here past 7 o'clock. How about we try it for a few weeks and see how it goes? We'll need to give staff and customers advance notice, but I say, go for it."

Her phone buzzed, interrupting her response. "It's HB."

***

HB quickly found the bookstore and parked as close as possible. The wipers couldn't keep up with the driving rain and it was hard for him to see if Charlotte was near the door. A movement caught his eye. There she was!

He cranked up the heat, left the car running and dashed through puddles to the store entrance. Opening the main door he found her, soaked and shivering, hunched as far into the corner as she could get.

A departing customer took one look at her, grimaced in distaste and gave her as wide a berth as possible. A jab of reality for him to never judge by appearances.

"Let's get you out of here. The car's right outside." He reached for her arm.

Through chattering teeth Charlotte spoke. "Thank you. I'm safe now, right?"

HB nodded and led her back to his car. He had a jacket in the back seat and tucked it around her.

"I'm g...g...getting your car all wet. S... sorry."

He waved off her concern. "It needs cleaning anyway. More important to get you warmed up and dry. Your mother will be happy to know you're safe."

She jerked around to face him. "I'm not going back there! Please – HB. Please don't take me back there."

"Okay, okay. Calm down. Tell me what happened?"

While he waited for her to answer, he wondered about the only possible safe haven he could take her. He couldn't tell if those were tears running down her face, or water dripping from her hair. Poor kid, all her toughness had melted with the rain, and he easily imagined how she'd been as a younger child. But if this kind of anxiety-ridden territory went with being a parent, he was grateful to have missed out. Or was he?

She'd stopped shivering and began wiping her face with her sleeve. HB reached into the glove compartment and handed her a wad of unused fast-food napkins. "This might help."

"He scared me so much," she said, dabbing at her hair and face.

"Who did, Charlotte? You're safe now. I won't let anyone hurt you. I promise."

Finally, a weak smile from his passenger. "I know you won't. That's why I called you." A small sob escaped. "It was Uncle Xander. I've never seen him like that. I had to run away. I think he must know something about what happened to my dad."

A fresh round of tears flowed. Time to get her away from here. "Listen, take your time. I do need to let the police know you're safe though. They have a lot of people looking for you, who'd be better off now looking for your dad, right?"

She nodded.

HB punched in Keleher's number. She answered on the first ring. "Keleher."

"It's HB. I want to let you know I've found Charlotte and she's safe with me. She doesn't want to go home, so I'm going to take her to Dorothy for safe keeping." For the time being he'd leave out the fact she'd been terrified of Xander, at least until he got the full story.

"Put this on speaker." HB complied. "Charlotte? This is Sergeant Shelby Keleher. I'm glad you're safe. Do you need any medical attention?"

"No, I'm okay, now."

"Good. And can you confirm for me you are willing, and agree, to go with Mr. Bartholomew?"

"Yes. He's the only one I feel safe with."

"That's fine, Charlotte. Thank you. HB – please give me the location where you and Charlotte will be. I will come and talk with you both there."

HB provided directions to Maxwell's and disconnected the call. He hoped he would have a chance to get all the story from Charlotte before Keleher arrived on the scene. He put the car in drive and pulled away from the curb. Some days he really hated the rain Portland got - the days it never seemed to end.

"So, I'm taking you to where my boss, Dorothy Dennehy, works. You've met her back at the house, remember? She owns a restaurant in a marina. It won't be busy this time of the evening ..."

Charlotte looked at him, panic flashing across her face. "What time is it?"

HB gritted his teeth. "It's just gone six."

"So why didn't that police person say if the ransom has been paid. Maybe my dad is home now?"

"I've always been upfront with you, you know that, right?"

She could only nod, her wide, water-filled eyes threatening to spill over.

"If there had been good news, she would have told us just now, don't you think? But, hey, I could be wrong. Maybe she hasn't heard anything yet either. By the time we get to Dorothy's we'll probably have an update. In the meantime, while we drive, tell me what happened." He stole a quick glance at her profile. Her lower lip trembled – he needed her to be distracted. "Did you find your uncle, or was it the other way round?"

"I wanted to go into the one coffee shop I know Dad likes, to ask if they'd seen him, but Uncle Xander saw me first before I could go in. He looked about to go ballistic - his face all red, and his eyes were so mean! I wasn't sure what to do, but he moved so fast. He made me get into his car, and he put my bike in his trunk. We didn't drive too far. It looked like an alley close to where I was. He wasn't talking, and he kept hitting his hand against the steering wheel. I've never seen him like that."

While he considered what she said, the blasting air from the car heater and the slap of the windshield wipers were the only sounds in the car. Xander had to be in this up to his eyeballs – had he kidnapped Etienne? How much was Olivia involved in this? His thoughts were interrupted when his phone rang.

"Jordan – what news?"

"The police have given up on the ransom drop. It's nearly six-thirty and no one has come for the money. They're in there now, taking it back. Where are you?"

Charlotte shrieked. "But my dad! What's happened? Is he ... dead?"

"Is that Charlotte? Sh ..., sorry man. I didn't think she was with you. I wouldn't have said anything ..."

"It's done now. We're heading over to the marina and Maxwell's. Meet us there."

The call ended and HB tried to get Charlotte back on track. "We'll get more info from him in a few minutes. We're nearly there. Jordan was the one who found your bike, and your backpack. He's one of my team trying to find your dad." He risked a side look at the distraught girl. "Listen, we have not given up. Got it?"

She could only nod as she wiped at a new trail of black mascara running down her face.

"After you got to the alley, what happened?"

"He yelled at me for leaving the house. Said I'd probably ruined everything. Why would he say that? I never did anything to make him mad before. And I was so happy when he came back after Dad was taken ..." Her voice grew stronger. "Do you think he ...?"

"Let's not jump to conclusions for the moment, okay? What else did he say?"

"I couldn't always make out what he was saying. He swore so much. He wouldn't answer any of my questions. When we stopped in the alley, he told me to stay put. He got out, opened the trunk and tried to toss my bike into a dumpster. That's when I got really scared and left the car to get away. He grabbed me, hard. I slipped and my shoe came off. He yanked at my shoulder, but I guess that's when he only got my backpack instead because I got free, and I ran and ran."

"I'm glad you got away. He sounds like a very angry man."

The tears had dried up and Charlotte tensed in the seat beside him. "Yeah, well he didn't look all that angry anytime I saw him and my mother being cuddle buddies. Gross."

"Before your mother left your father?"

"No. Since my dad was kidnapped! I caught them twice when they thought I didn't see them. Wrapped around each other like snakes. Tongues and all. Epic gross."

HB flinched. She could be crude, but he got the picture. "I had the impression they were no longer, um, involved."

"I bet that's what they want people to think." She tugged angrily at her seatbelt. "When do we get wherever it is you're taking me?"

"Almost there. Any idea where your uncle has gone?"

"Nope, and I don't care." She slammed back against the seat, crossing her arms across her chest.

HB figured now was the time to actually let Dorothy know he was bringing Charlotte to her. He commanded his hands-free screen to call her. "Boss, I have Charlotte. We're heading your way. Put lots of coffee on and grab some towels. Oh, Keleher and Jordan should be there soon too."

CHAPTER TWENTY-FOUR

The rain began to ease as HB reached Maxwell's. He glanced over at Charlotte, she stared, stone-faced, out the window, chewing on what was left of her chipped, black nails.

"This will all work out, you'll see. We'll find your dad and then things will get back to normal." HB's lack of experience with teens made him worry his platitudes weren't getting through. Or worse, would seem lip service. The bedraggled girl seemed determined to keep further tears at bay, when she blurted out what was likely uppermost in her mind. "How can you say that? He's been gone forever. Back to normal? What's that? Dad kidnapped, my supposed uncle has turned ugly and my stupid mother ... I never want to see either of them again."

Her anger was palpable, but HB preferred that to tears. He kept his tone level, ignoring the outburst. "Here we are." He parked the car, turned off the engine and looked at her.

"Charlotte, we're at the marina now, and this is Maxwell's Bar and Grill. I promise, you'll be safe here."

She leaned forward to have a better look at the haven she'd been brought to. HB waited. What if she didn't want to go inside? He couldn't force her. So, he tried another tactic.

"I don't know about you, but I could sure do with something hot to drink. And I bet you'd be ready to have something to eat by now as well. C'mon. Let's go. I'm sure Dorothy will have something for you to change into. You've had quite an ordeal and Sergeant Keleher will want to ask questions. They are working hard to find him, you know, which means anything you can tell them will help."

A shrug was all he got. But then she reached for the handle and opened the door. He breathed a sigh of relief. "I'm sure Dorothy can find you something for your feet. Let's get you dry and warm before the cops arrive. Deal?"

Charlotte turned to him, eyes narrowed and her jaw set. "I trust you, HB. What do you think? Has Uncle Xander done this - has he killed my dad? And my mother? Where does she fit in all this.?" Her venting complete, she took a deep breath and her face relaxed. A small smile pushed away the worry on her face and a note of shyness crept into her voice. "Thank you, again, for finding me. You'd make a great dad."

She'd done it to him again. Left him speechless. Damn. He took her elbow. "Let's get you inside and we can talk all about it and what we can do to find your father." HB guided her, hopping on her shoed foot, through the front door of Maxwell's.

As they came in through the doors, HB was grateful there were no customers on hand. He'd get Dorothy, or Rolin, to put up the closed sign soon as Shelby and Jordan arrived. Charlotte didn't need any curious patrons giving her the once over. He spied Dorothy coming around from behind the bar. She held towels and her welcoming smile brought his anxiety level down.

***

HB nodded at Rolin as he joined Dorothy. There'd been little conversation other than to ensure Charlotte was warmed up, and fed. Dorothy had found her a pair of sneakers in the lost and found box that fit and offered her an old sweatshirt she kept at the bar. Charlotte sipped on a cup of hot cocoa and soon devoured a burger and fries.

HB couldn't believe someone her size could practically inhale so much food. "I hope that helps warm your insides, Charlotte. Do you need anything else?"

She wiped her fingers and pushed the empty plate away. "Thanks. I was so hungry, and that was an epic burger. Could I have a glass of water, with some lemon?"

"I'll get it," said Rolin as Dorothy got up. "You sit and talk with her. The others will be here any minute, right?"

HB stood back. This was Dorothy's show now and he could see she was concerned for Charlotte as the girl spoke. "But what's going to happen to me now? I can't just sit here. I need to keep looking for him. Like I told HB, I'm not going back to the house until he's found. You can't make me!"

Dorothy sat beside her, putting her arm around the young girl. "Charlotte, you're with friends here and we'll look after you until you can be reunited with your dad. You'll meet my dad and stepmother in a while and, if you like, you can stay with them while we continue to search for him."

Charlotte looked at HB as if for advice, and he gave her a thumbs up. "Yes, okay, but it won't be for long, will it?"

"We'll hope it's only for a short while. Now what else can you tell us about what happened with your Uncle Xander?"

Any further discussion with Charlotte came to an end as Shelby and Jordan arrived.

"Boss. Maybe putting up the closed sign would be a good idea now?"

Shelby acknowledged Dorothy with a curt, "Good idea, HB. If you wouldn't mind, Dorothy."

Dorothy raised an eyebrow at HB as she moved past him to comply. She came back and stood beside him as Shelby approached Charlotte.

"So, you're Charlotte. We spoke on the phone. I'm Sergeant Keleher and I'm glad to meet you. You're still sure you don't need a doctor?

"No, I'm fine. HB, and everyone, has been looking after me. Oh, I know you, I've seen you at my house." Then she raised her voice and demanded, "Why haven't you found my father yet? This has gone on too long and if it wasn't for HB I wouldn't even be here. I think he should be in charge."

Dorothy intervened to calm the waters. "It doesn't work that way, Charlotte. HB and I are a private investigation company, but the police are in charge of this case. We're involved because Xander asked us to — well let's just say it's become complicated. Why don't you tell all of us what happened when your uncle found you in the Mystic district?"

"Again? I suppose so."

HB stayed silent while she reiterated what he already knew, but he watched Shelby pay careful attention to her, taking notes and occasionally asking Charlotte to clarify a point. He was impressed by the consideration she gave to Charlotte. As did Dorothy. He looked over at Jordan, who'd been silent since arriving. Shelby might have questions for him, but in the meantime, it appeared his protege was in observation mode. A good trait for an investigator to cultivate.

Shelby put her pen down. "Well done, Charlotte, thank you. Not a nice experience for you. Are you sure you have no idea where your uncle would go? Did he say anything, no matter how insignificant, that might help us find him - or even what he might be planning next?"

HB bit down on a smile forming when he recognized Charlotte's typical *are you out of your mind* look that she shot at Shelby. Her tone was laced with sarcasm. "Sergeant, I was scared and trying to escape. So no, he didn't inform me of his next moves."

"Of course."

HB caught Shelby's eye and he gave a shrug just as her phone chirped. "Keleher. Right, right, I'll be at the station shortly and in the meantime put out an APB on Xander Michelson's car. Proceed with caution but we need to find him."

"We're here now, darlin'. How can we help? This must be Charlotte."

HB turned. Max and Alanna had arrived unnoticed. HB moved over to Charlotte as Dorothy introduced Charlotte to them. He wanted her to feel at ease with them. "You trust me, right? So, these are two of the best people I know, and you'll be in good hands with them. Only for a short while. Max here is a great cook, and if you liked that burger before, well, you're in for a treat."

Charlotte glanced cautiously between him and the new couple on the scene. "But you'll keep in touch as soon as anything happens?"

HB crossed his heart. "You know I will. Go on now."

Charlotte shrugged and HB thought she looked defeated. "You need some sleep. Things will look better in the morning."

Shelby took down details of where Charlotte was going and remained silent until the trio had left the bar.

***

Rolin watched them go. He'd never had children. His ex-wife had been adamant children didn't interest her. Throughout the years as an international criminal lawyer, he'd mentored many young people who were interested in the law. He saw a spark in Charlotte that could be developed. He would talk with HB about her when this was all over.

He spent a moment observing the sergeant - the call she'd received seemed urgent, but yet she stayed. She had her back to him as they stood at the bar watching Charlotte leave with the Dennehys. After rearranging coasters on the bar, he extended his hand, realizing they'd hadn't been introduced. "Good to put a face to a name, Sergeant. I'm Rolin Montase, Dorothy's business partner here at Maxwell's."

Keleher returned the handshake, the neutral expression on her face giving nothing away. "Good to meet you, Mr. Montase. I believe you also still practice law here at the Marina? Always helps to know of a good lawyer."

Before he had a chance to answer, Shelby turned her focus to HB, and Dorothy. "I'll head back to the precinct now. However, one last thing. I know HB is probably aware, but the ransom drop at the laundromat was never picked up. We have the funds locked up and they will be returned to the Rivard home at the conclusion of this case."

Dorothy's shoulders sagged and she closed her eyes at the news and its implications.

Rolin wondered how this case would turn out. It wasn't looking hopeful at this point. He kept his thoughts to himself as the sergeant continued. "And here's a nugget for you. It appears Mr. Michelson is the owner of the laundromat, as well as the units above it."

Her phone chirped again. "Keleher. What! On my way."

She began to run for the door. "We've had an anonymous tip that Etienne can be found in one of those units! HB - you're welcome to come along."

Rolin stood next to Dorothy as they watched HB race after Keleher. "He didn't need to be asked twice, did he?"

Dorothy nudged him. "And look at Jordan. I don't think he knows what to do. I'll have a word."

She spoke to Jordan. "You can follow them if you like, but don't get in the way, got it? And make sure I hear back from you or HB the minute there is news - of any kind!"

And then the bar was empty except for him and Dorothy. They looked at each other until she spoke. "And now we wait. Have I told you before that's the worst part of this business?"

He managed to stand a little closer to her, so their shoulders touched. "And I'm waiting right here with you. Although I have to say, I prefer the law. This side of investigations — the anxiety — is not for me. So guess I don't much like waiting either. Present company helps."

She turned to face him. They stood so close the pulse in her neck was visible, and he yearned to pull her even closer. He forced himself to pull back. "How about a bottle of something red while we wait?"

CHAPTER TWENTY-FIVE

Dorothy's phone rang. "Dad. What's wrong?"

"No worries, darlin'. Thought you might want to know the colleen is doing just fine. Alanna found some clothes for her, and right now she's got her face planted in her phone. We'll leave her be for a bit. Any news, then?"

"Not yet, but the minute I do, I'll be in touch. Once Rolin and I close up here, I'll be home. Thanks again for taking her in. HB's right, she seems tough as nails on the outside, but she really needs her dad, and it shows." She paused. "If he's as good a dad as you are, then for her sake I hope he's found alive."

"Have a little faith, my girl," said Max. "You keep in touch. We won't be sleeping till we hear from you."

She disconnected the call and put the phone down on the table. The bottle of red, half-full, sat between her and Rolin.

"All good on the home front?" he asked.

"For now." She put a stopper in the bottle. "One glass is enough. I'll be heading home shortly. Wish we'd hear from HB."

She watched the smile play around his mouth. Truth be told, while she was concerned about the case, she also wanted time alone to think about what she was feeling right now. Standing next to Rolin at the bar had been fine. Until their shoulders touched. She'd felt a current jolt something inside her. Something that had been locked down tight since Paul's death.

"You're a million miles away, Dee."

"Sorry, what?"

"I asked you to keep in touch when you leave here. I'm anxious to hear as well. Charlotte has a lot riding on the safe return of her father."

Dorothy stood. "She does. Time to clear out of here. The minute I hear anything, I'll call."

***

A few miles away in Portland proper, car doors slammed, and feet rushed through the laundromat to the back door exit. HB, and Jordan, followed Keleher and three uniforms up the less than sturdy wooden steps to a locked door. HB briefly noted three apartment numbers listed on the door. Which unit was Etienne in? They'd better get it right the first time.

Keleher nodded at one of her team and with one mighty kick the locked door flew open. A door to their right cracked open and a startled face peered out at them. "Back inside," barked Keleher.

They stopped outside a door. "Number three – this is it." Keleher held up a hand for silence and she leaned her head against the door to listen. Then she took two steps back and rammed her shoulder against the flimsy wooden door which gave way with a splintering of the wooden frame.

HB stretched on tip toes to see over shoulders. The interior was in darkness - eerily quiet. Were they too late? Was Etienne dead? He thought of Charlotte and his stomach twisted.

Flashlights came on and pierced the darkness, and as the group moved into the apartment, they began to spread out. HB knew enough to not interfere, and he laid his hand on Jordan, but his whole being wanted to rush from room to room until he found Charlotte's father.

"Sarge! Over here!"

She moved ahead, hand already on her shoulder mic, calling for an ambulance. Then she was kneeling beside a grimy mattress, resting on a piece of heavy carpeting, where Etienne lay. HB pushed forward, his gut in knots until Etienne's mouth twitched and eyelids fluttered open. One wrist was handcuffed to an old radiator and both feet were shackled as well. Empty water bottles lay scattered about.

"Get forensics here. Soon as Mr. Rivard is in an ambulance, I want this place gone over inch by inch." An officer moved away to carry out her command. "And somebody get back outside to wait for the bus."

In a kinder tone of voice than HB expected, she spoke to the kidnap victim. "Mr. Rivard. We have an ambulance on the way." She reached for her handcuff key and undid his restraints. He tried to sit up, and HB reached forward to offer support.

"Charlotte," Etienne rasped. "Where is she? Is she okay?"

"Mr. Rivard, your daughter is well and safe. Right now, we need to get you taken care of." Even as she spoke HB detected an approaching siren.

Etienne sank back against HB's arm, barely conscious. Questions would have to wait. The guy was spent. Probably hadn't had much to eat in days and needed a change of clothes. Soon as they had him on the way to the hospital, he'd let Charlotte know her dad was safe.

Poor guy had been held here for more than a week. Brutal. Only a mattress and a thin blanket. Garbage in the kitchen showed a few fast-food wrappers but didn't seem like much for a week. How often had his captor brought him anything to eat, and worse, allowed him use of the toilet?

A small kitchen table and two chairs was it for the kitchen. HB couldn't see much of the bedroom, but he could see a dresser and the footboard of a bed. A real bed, but yet Etienne was confined to the mattress in the living room. Windows had heavy duty blinds pulled all the way down, and the light in the kitchen was low wattage.

The carpeting under the mattress would have muffled any sounds Etienne might have tried to make, but the noisy laundromat below would have disguised most of it anyway. Someone had thought ahead. And that someone had to be Xander. No doubt about it now.

Shelby continued to speak gently to Etienne and HB was aware she hadn't mentioned Xander by name, and he knew enough to keep quiet about it as well. All they had now was circumstantial evidence, but assuming Etienne had seen him, it would soon be confirmed.

HB clenched his fists, angry on Charlotte's behalf that someone she trusted would put her through this. The cops better find him first, or Stonefist Sandy would be no match for HB's righteous anger.

Paramedics arrived, and HB stood off to one side to let them work. He walked over to where Jordan stood, observing, but his face mirrored the disgust and anger HB felt. "Will he be okay, HB?"

"I don't know, Jordan. When we finish here, I'm going to see Charlotte, if it's not too late, and I want you to write up your account on what you've seen, what you've observed.

Record any questions you have that can't be answered. Facts, not feelings – got it?"

"You've got it. I'll send it to you before I call it a day."

They stood to one side as the paramedics, their patient loaded on the stretcher, left the apartment. An oxygen mask covered most of Etienne's face and his eyes stayed closed. HB said a silent prayer to whoever might be listening that the guy would be okay. He had a daughter who needed him. Now more than ever.

He shot Dorothy a text.

Etienne found. On my way to see you.

***

Dorothy was ready to answer the door when the knock came. It was nearly midnight, but sleep would be postponed a while yet. She'd left a message for Rolin, and her dad that Etienne was safe. She opened the door and HB closed it behind him.

"Is Charlotte awake?" HB asked.

"No, she finally went to sleep about an hour ago from what I heard. I think we should let her sleep for a few hours before telling her he's been found. It gives some time for a medical update as well. Sounds like he was found none too soon. What a scumbag Xander is."

"My thoughts too, Boss. Xander better hope the cops find him before we do ... or even Charlotte! The kid's had way too many disappointing adults in her life."

"Come through to the kitchen. I put coffee on after you texted me."

One small light lent the kitchen a cozy feel as they sat at the kitchen table. "I can fix you a sandwich if you're hungry?"

"Coffee's fine. I think I'd feel guilty eating after seeing the lack of food for Etienne."

"Shelby called me as well. To bring me up to date. She asked if I'd be seeing you anytime soon. I didn't let on it would be this soon. I still say she has an interest in you, my friend."

HB sputtered over a gulp of his coffee, and Dorothy was sure there was mutual attraction.

"Never mind that for now," she nearly giggled. "More important matters at hand. Do you think Xander might have been the anonymous tipster?"

"Had to be him, Boss. Last action of a guilty conscience, maybe. Whatever. Cops have pulled out all the stops to find him, and I'll be working on a plan as well. I'd like to talk with Charlotte before the police try to pump her for more information. She probably knows things she doesn't realize."

HB recounted details of Etienne's rescue. Dorothy's notebook, never far away, soon had pages filled with notes, and questions she'd want resolved.

"And just how much is Olivia involved? There has to be a connection," she said, laying her pen aside. She blinked and fought back a yawn.

"Oh, she's involved all right. I need to do some digging and compare notes with Keleher perhaps. She's a piece of work. Olivia, not Keleher."

Dorothy laughed and gathered up empty mugs. "Time to call it a night." She glanced at the wall clock. "I'll get Charlotte up for seven a.m., if she's not up before."

"I'd like to be the one to tell her, Boss. If possible."

"And I agree, so how about you take the guest room for what's left of the night?" She saw indecision move across his face. "I'm still your boss, so you're staying!"

HB groaned, "Uncle."

CHAPTER TWENTY-SIX

The early morning news played across Dorothy's TV in her living room when HB came down the stairs yawning and stretching. "Charlotte not up yet? Poor kid must be exhausted. Can I grab a coffee before I talk to her?"

Dorothy murmured a good morning. "Help yourself. There's a fresh pot in the kitchen. Oh, look. Shelby's on the news making a statement."

HB's head swiveled to watch the sergeant; coffee forgotten. He sat on the sofa beside Dorothy, who didn't miss the intense focus HB gave to the uniformed woman on the screen. Shelby tapped the microphone, cleared her throat, and began to speak in a controlled voice as she launched into a statement concerning Etienne's rescue. "I'll keep this brief as this is still an ongoing investigation. At 10.00 last night, after an anonymous call, we located Etienne Rivard, the owner of Michard Estates Winery. Mr. Rivard had been missing, and we believe may have been kept hostage, for eight days. He is now recovering in hospital. Further details of his condition will be forthcoming, and we ask you respect his family's privacy at this time."

Voices from the press began to pepper her with questions, and she held up a hand for silence as she continued. "We are extremely interested to speak with Xander Michelson in connection with this investigation."

A photo of Michelson came up on screen, along with a phone number.

Cameras flashed and reporters jostled for Keleher's attention. "There will be no questions taken at this time, but

I would ask the public that if they have any information concerning the whereabouts of Xander Michelson, then call us at the number shown on the screen or contact their local police department."

Excited voices rose in pitch, trying to outshout each other to get her attention.

"And yet they continue to try and ask questions." observed HB as the camera followed Keleher and her aide move away from the scrum of reporters.

Dorothy tapped the remote, and silence returned to her living room. "I give her credit for knowing how to handle the press."

HB stood. "Right, now I'll get my coffee."

As he turned toward the kitchen, he stopped short when Charlotte appeared.

"Morning Charlotte. Sorry, we didn't hear you come in. And I was just on my way to give you the good news. Do Alanna and Max know you're up?"

She still looked a little sleep-dazed and nodded. "They're not up yet but showed me the way in here before I went to bed last night." She blinked and looked from HB to Dorothy. "Is she right? The police sergeant? Dad's really okay?"

Dorothy let HB respond to the teenager. She didn't want to interfere with the bond HB had built with her. The concern on his face as he moved closer to Charlotte was genuine.

The young girl was still in the pajamas Alanna had found for her. Her hair was matted like a bird's nest and her eyes barely open, but the hug she gave HB meant she didn't care how she looked, and her smile spoke volumes.

"It's true, then - it's really true! When can I see him? And I should tell Uncle Max and Aunt Alanna!"

Dorothy smiled at her, "Uncle and Aunt? You must have made a good impression. I'm sure they'll be up shortly, and you can give them the good news yourself."

"They asked me to call them that. You're so lucky to have parents like them." A cloud passed over her face. "You've met my mother. She's a bitch and I hate her!"

Dorothy was disturbed at the flash change in Charlotte. From joy at hearing about Etienne to full-on vehemence against her mother. "She's still your mother, and maybe you don't know the whole story that's made her who she is?"

Charlotte unclenched the fists she'd held at her side. "Maybe. Whatever." Then she turned to HB. "Can you take me to the hospital now - you promised you would as soon as he was found. I need to see him!"

Dorothy waited to see how HB would handle this.

His voice was calm, but not patronizing. "Hang on a minute. I understand you're anxious to see him and I will take you, but first I need to talk with Sergeant Keleher. They're likely with him right now with tons of questions."

Disappointment dimmed her excitement. "But not too much later, please!" Then she looked down. "Crap - I can't wear this to the hospital.

It was time for Dorothy to step in. "First things first. Breakfast. I don't know about you, but I'm hungry. And I'm pretty sure HB can put together one of his famous omelets for us."

HB sputtered. "Famous? I don't know about omelets, but I can do scrambled and toast. Yes - please hold the applause - I'm a wiz at making toast." He bent low at the waist.

Once again HB surprised Dorothy when Charlotte actually giggled at his performance.

A quiet knock interrupted the levity, and Dorothy welcomed Alanna, who came bearing a pile of freshly laundered clothes for Charlotte.

"Perfect timing," said Dorothy. "Thanks, Alanna. Charlotte, why don't you have a shower and get dressed? By then breakfast will be ready."

***

Twenty minutes later a well-fed group sat at Dorothy's kitchen table. Max and Alanna had joined them for breakfast. Dorothy held her comments - the look on her dad's face as they sampled HB's so-so scrambled eggs was priceless. The slightly burnt toast was accompanied by endless glasses of orange juice for all.

As the meal finished, Max offered to take Charlotte to the hospital.

"Thank you, Uncle Max, but HB promised to take me." She zeroed in on HB. "You've talked to the sergeant by now, right?"

"Yes, we have the all clear. Let's go."

Charlotte faced them all, a tentative smile on her face. "You know, maybe I should be a private investigator when I grow up."

***

HB and Charlotte were on their way to the hospital, leaving Alanna and Max to help with clean up. When they left, it allowed Dorothy quiet time to contemplate the bond HB and Charlotte had. The respect she showed for HB contradicted her mercurial mood swings. One moment angry at the world, the next showing understanding and a maturity beyond her years which made her infinitely more likeable. HB had become her champion and role model. The kid could do worse.

Dorothy wondered if she'd put her own dad through a similar emotional roller coaster when she'd been that age. Probably. She'd have to ask. And it looked as if Etienne would be bringing up a teenage daughter by himself, just as her dad had done.

She chided herself for lazing about and moved to her bedroom to dress for work. She knew the Vineyard Case, as they'd nicknamed it, was in good hands with HB. He'd keep her up to date as would Shelby. But, as she brushed her long hair, the frustration she felt over the man who'd engineered this whole scenario came to the surface. She tossed the brush aside with the thought that she probably wouldn't be paid if he went to jail. Her pragmatic side realized she'd likely have to write the loss off to experience.

Thirty minutes later, she arrived at Maxwell's and found Rolin in the loading dock area, shifting kegs of beer. He looked up at her arrival. "Morning Dee. My first appointment was canceled, so I thought I'd help out with this delivery."

Seeing him first thing was a pleasant surprise. "Morning to you as well. I knew I'd picked the right partner for this business, but could you leave that for now? Tables need to be set for the lunch crowd. Although, seeing you're there, can you bring out a half dozen bottles of the red that's become so popular."

"That would be the Pinot Noir from Michard Estates?"

She nodded but couldn't keep a sardonic note from her voice. "Yes, it's always been popular but now it seems to have reached cult status. I do hope Etienne Rivard will be able to return to his business. They're a good supplier, always on time with their orders, and the wine is superior."

Rolin set the bottles on the bar. She knew what he was thinking before he said it. "Yes, I know, Rolin. You don't have to say it. I would rather be in the thick of things right now. So, you need to help me keep busy and not think about it!"

He laughed and moved to prep the tables for hungry customers. "Right, no need to mention HB will be in touch when he has news. Got it."

"And surprise, you just did." Dorothy giggled. "Thanks for keeping me in line, sir!"

She gave him a mock salute and focused on restocking the bar.

CHAPTER TWENTY-SEVEN

"Relax, Charlotte. I'm not going to drive any faster. Look, the hospital is up ahead."

It took a while for HB to find parking, but they finally made their way inside, found the elevators, and the floor where Charlotte's father was under medical care. Police presence outside his room made it easy to find.

Charlotte jumped ahead, anxious to reach him. She skidded to a stop outside the door, halted by the officer on duty. "I want to see him!"

HB threw a glance at the uniform and explained the reason for their presence. "One sec, let me talk to the sarge." A quick tap on the door and the officer poked his head inside. He backed up as a doctor came out of the room, closing the door behind him. But not moving away. HB was pretty sure he'd sized up the state of impatience Charlotte was in.

"You are Mr. Rivard's daughter? I'm the doctor in charge of his care. Your father is awake, and you can see him ..." Charlotte made for the door, until HB grabbed her arm. "But he is weak and needs a lot of rest." Then his stern face softened. "Your dad is anxious to see you as well. Just don't overtire him. Understand?"

Charlotte nodded, but HB knew she was ready to fly into the room. He acknowledged the doctor's advice. "Thanks, doc. I'll see to it she behaves. Police still talking with him?"

"Yes. She, the officer in charge, wants to stay in the room while Charlotte sees him. She's said you may be there as well." The doctor moved away from the door. "Go ahead."

Charlotte now hesitated and looked to HB, and only when HB tipped his head toward the door did she quietly push it open. HB followed behind.

He dreaded hospitals. The smells, the equipment. The last one he'd been in saw him leave with stitches and crutches. He only did this for Charlotte. So, he'd have to suck it up.

Charlotte came to a dead stop. No running to jump on the bed, or bear-hug her father. And no wonder. This was HB's first good look at the kidnap victim. Too much activity, and crappy lighting, around his rescue the night before hadn't given him much chance. Judging by Charlotte's reaction, he was in bad shape. His sunken eyes were closed, and a scruffy beard barely disguised bruising around his neck. Corded veins on his arms highlighted weight loss. IV lines were in place to replace fluids, but it would take a while to put some meat on those bones.

It was the beeping of machines HB hated the most. To lie there and be aware that each beep meant you were still alive, ready to panic if the noise stopped.

Charlotte had stepped closer to the bed. "Dad?" she whispered. "It's me. Open your eyes. Please."

HB glanced over at Shelby Keleher. Her eyes glistened, and she stepped closer to HB in order to talk quietly with him. "He can't stay awake long. I only need a couple more questions answered and then we can let him rest. But Michelson's on the run and time's working against us."

HB warred with himself. Talk to Keleher outside the room and find out the latest or stay in case Charlotte needed him. He smirked to himself. When was the last time two very different females vied for his attention?

He decided to stay. With luck, he'd accomplish both tasks at the same time.

"Dad?"

HB watched Charlotte grab the bruised hand nearest her. The patient's fingers tightened around hers, his eyes twitched, then blinked.

Standing next to him, Shelby Keleher let out a pent-up breath. "Thank God," she whispered. She leaned closer to HB. "I was afraid he wouldn't come around for his daughter. But look."

Charlotte clung to her dad's arm. "I knew you'd be found. Did Uncle Xander do this to you?"

Rivard licked his lips. His voice a whisper "Slow down, girl. Are you okay? What about your mother?"

Charlotte stiffened. "She'd better not come anywhere near you. I hate her and we don't need her. When do you come home?"

HB stepped in. "Charlotte. Maybe leave some of the questions until your dad is feeling better?"

Rivard focused on HB. "And you are?"

Charlotte jumped in. "Dad – this is HB. He's the best investigator. Even better than the police. He saved me from Uncle Xander and I'm staying with his boss's parents until you're better."

It was all too much for Etienne and he sank back against the pillows, his eyes closed.

"Charlotte," said Keleher, "We need to let him rest. The doctors say he will be fine, but he needs time to heal. Let's leave him be for now, alright?"

HB looked at Shelby. "Thought you had more questions for him?"

Shelby tipped her head toward Charlotte. "My questions can wait for a bit. This was more important. Let's go."

HB opened the door, crooked his finger at Charlotte, and mouthed, "Let him rest."

In the hallway, Keleher had a suggestion HB readily agreed to. "I know you both have lots of questions. There's a coffee shop downstairs. I can provide some answers." She looked at Charlotte. "If you want, Charlotte. I know I'm not high on your list of favorites right now, so I'd like to try and rectify that."

When Charlotte looked at HB, he kept a neutral tone. "Good idea. Even if the coffee's probably awful."

A few minutes later, the three found seats in the busy spot. HB had requested water with a slice of lemon for Charlotte, much to the surprised look on Shelby's face.

She didn't waste time. "So, this is what I can tell you, mostly from what your father has been able to tell us so far."

Charlotte grasped her drink tightly in both hands, eyes wide and focused on Shelby.

"As you know. — and I am sorry, Charlotte — Xander Michelson is our chief suspect in the kidnapping of your father. At this point your father can't confirm it because his abductor never showed his face and used a voice-distortion apparatus for any conversations. His memory is hazy, but he wonders if a second person was involved as well."

HB wasn't surprised. He'd bet they'd find Olivia's prints at the hovel where Etienne had been restrained. Before he could comment Charlotte jumped to her own conclusion.

"That Frisco Butler guy, right? He had a ransom note on him, so I thought he was the one who took Dad?"

"We have yet to clarify the connection there. On the surface, yes, it would appear Mr. Butler was involved, but as to how much, we don't know. And prefer not to speculate."

"So, when Butler was killed, someone still had to be making the demands. He had at least one other partner, then?" Charlotte covered all the angles.

"Possibly, yes."

HB smiled. "Charlotte might be young, but she's impressed me with her knowledge of how crimes are structured and criminal behavior in general."

Charlotte beamed at HB. "You showed me tons as well." She turned to Keleher. "I might just be a private investigator when I grow up."

"Or the police force?"

Charlotte shook her head. "Too many rules."

HB thought it would be a good time to move this train to another track. "Tell us, Sergeant, were you able to learn anything else from Mr. Rivard?"

"Not a great deal about the abduction itself. The last thing your father remembers is having a coffee in the Mystic District. He'd nearly finished it, when he began to feel unwell. He thought he was going to faint and tried to call for help. Someone helped him to his feet, he heard the person say something like, "My friend is unwell, I'll get him home." And that's it. When he came to, he was in the apartment where we found him, restrained and alone."

HB's phone buzzed, and he read a text from Jordan. "Shel ... Sergeant. Here's something one of my guys found out. Not sure you were aware, but Michelson rented a car a week before Mr. Rivard's kidnap and then returned it to the agency the day after."

Shelby made a note. "I hadn't been aware of this, thank you."

A nurse in scrubs approached their table. "Are you connected with Etienne Rivard?"

Charlotte jumped to her feet. "That's my dad – has something happened?"

The nurse smiled. "No, it's okay. If you're Charlotte, your dad is asking for you." Then she looked at the uniformed Sergeant. "If that's alright?"

Shelby nodded and waved Charlotte away. "Go already. I'll give you a few minutes, but then I'm coming back up, so don't tire him out again. Please."

Charlotte raced ahead of the nurse toward the elevators, leaving HB alone with Shelby.

"Another?" he asked, pointing to her empty cup.

"I'll pass, thanks. Listen, HB. Now Charlotte's out of range there are a couple of things I can share with you she doesn't need to know right now."

"It's her mother, I bet. The ever-charming Olivia?"

"No wonder you're a good investigator," Shelby laughed, then grew serious. "I didn't want Charlotte to know, but her mother is at the station, waiting to be questioned in relation to this crime."

"You think she's involved?"

"I'm sure she's involved. But to what extent isn't clear."

"I can see where Charlotte gets her mood swings from. That woman is a piece of work. Runs hot and cold. One minute she portrays herself as a victim, then she wants to be in control. I'm no social worker, but I see no value to Charlotte having Olivia in her life." He surprised himself at the anger he felt toward the woman who was Charlotte's mother. "The kid deserves a whole lot better than her."

"Not up to us to decide, though. Is it?" Shelby stood. "But here's another dot to connect. Paperwork has surfaced confirming Xander Michelson as owner of the laundromat and units above it. Done last year. More than a coincidence, I'd say, but wish we'd had that information days ago." She shoved the chair back against the table with enough force to make a woman sitting nearby jump. "Sorry," she offered to the startled customer. And then to HB, "I'm going back to see Mr. Rivard. I assume you want to come along?"

He didn't need to be asked a second time.

As they approached the hospital room, the doctor called to them from the nursing station. "Sergeant? I have the toxicology report." He read from a tablet. "Very high levels of Ketamine in Mr. Rivard's system. As if he's been given a continual low dose over a few days. His kidneys and liver are at risk, and we are running more tests, but I believe he was found before serious damage was done."

"Thank you, Doctor." As he returned to other duties, Shelby pulled HB aside. "Before we go in, I can tell you we learned Frisco Butler was known to deal in ketamine. He may have counted Xander Michelson as one of his contacts."

"Another couple of dots connected. I have some street connections, maybe I can find out more." He smiled. "Of course, you'll be informed."

Shelby held her hand on the door to Etienne's room. "I have to say, HB, before I met you, and Ms. Dennehy, I didn't have much regard for private investigators. But I've been impressed with your style." She tapped her fingers on the door handle. "Maybe, if you'd like, once this case is over, we could share some best practices."

"What, like over a dinner, you mean?" HB was annoyed that they both seemed to be so backward at coming forward. Shelby must be as out of touch as he was. Or she'd been hiding behind a uniform too long. And what had he been hiding behind?

"Yes. Dinner – or lunch. We'll set something up." She pushed the door open. It looked as if Etienne Rivard was once again out for the count. His daughter had pulled a chair as close to his bed as she could and was sound asleep, her arm wrapped around his.

They quietly backed out of the room. "I need to get back to the station. More questions here will have to wait." She looked at HB. "Do you want to come to the station and watch the interview with her mother?"

"You bet I would. But, let me make a phone call. Charlotte needs someone to get her home." He tapped his phone. "Max? I have a favor to ask."

CHAPTER TWENTY-EIGHT

HB stood behind the one-way glass watching Olivia St John-Rivard speaking with Sergeant Keleher. Shelby explained it was one of the less formal rooms used for interviews - not the stark intimidating space reserved for those arrested. The goal was to have Olivia feel relaxed as possible and perhaps catch her off-guard. But she was far from relaxed. Her tense body language matched her sullen face. And then, in the blink of an eye, it changed. HB shook his head at the chameleon in action as her demeanor softened and a smile — sly in his books — was directed at Shelby.

HB watched, curious to how this would proceed. He'd seen her play this game before, and knew Olivia put Olivia first. This would be new territory for Shelby, never having had the pleasure of Olivia's presence until now. The Sergeant had her back to him, so he couldn't gauge her facial reactions. He listened, as she methodically asked pertinent questions regarding the kidnap and especially her relationship with her former lover, Xander Michelson. Olivia's predictable response? She was no longer interested in the disgraced business owner of Michard Estates and didn't have a good word to say about him.

"I don't know what I ever saw in him. Hindsight and all that, you know. He was a good talker and I fell for his never-ending promises. I should have known better!"

"How do you account for information that, only recently, you and Xander Michelson shared intimate moments. Moments witnessed by your daughter."

"I have nothing to say on that. Charlotte is mistaken. You'd take the word of a child over me? Typical. I bet you don't have children, do you?"

Shelby didn't respond but moved her pen across her notebook. He longed to step in but knew he'd have to wait until invited.

"And where is Xander Michelson now?" Shelby looked up from her notebook and went for the direct approach.

"How many times do I have to tell you people? I don't know where he is, and I don't wish to talk about him. At all. I came here voluntarily, you know, but I'm beginning to feel like some kind of criminal. I can't get any kind of update on Etienne, or learn where the hell my daughter is!"

HB smirked. Shelby had managed to rattle her cage, not responding to any of Olivia's remarks. That should piss off Olivia in spades. Good.

Shelby looked up from her notepad at Olivia, then stood and walked to the door. "I'll be back in a moment Ms. St John-Rivard. We're not quite done, and I need a coffee." Turning back, she said, "Can I get you one?"

Olivia uncrossed her legs and shot daggers at Shelby. "No, I do not. How much longer is this going to take? I'd like to leave and take care of my daughter. Once I find her!"

"Just a little longer. Surely you realize one of the reasons we are talking with you is in the best interests of your daughter. I'll be right back, I still have one or two more questions."

HB admired Shelby's self-control and watched as she reached for the door's handle. Behind her, Olivia mouthed bitch as she left the room. Shelby joined HB outside the interview room.

"Going well, I see," said HB. "I think you got to her though with that last comment about Charlotte, judging by the silent nickname she had for you."

Keleher sighed in exasperation. "I can only imagine. She's something else."

They both turned to focus on the high-maintenance socialite who didn't try to hide her annoyance as she drummed her manicured nails on the table beside her.

"If she scowls any deeper, there won't be enough plastic surgery to erase those wrinkles," noted Shelby.

"Do you think she's really oblivious to knowing we can watch her?" asked HB.

She shrugged. "Don't know, don't care. What a frigging diva! Round two coming up and I'd like you in on it. You have a rapport, of sorts, with her and she might open up to you more than me. You game?"

HB ribbed. "Yeah, some kind of rapport is right. I don't know what I can get from her, but I'm willing to try. Appreciate you letting me give it a go."

"Only because this is an informal interview. You wouldn't have the opportunity if she was under arrest. But I think you may get more from her than I have so far."

"Especially now you've had the honor to experience her personality range. I don't for a second buy into any sincerity where her daughter is concerned. Olivia St John-Rivard is the poster child for 'me first'. Nasty woman. I'm, uh, sorry for what she called you. Undeserved. Her on the other hand? Well ..."

"Goes with the territory, HB. Believe me, I've been called worse. C'mon, let's get a coffee and discuss tactics before we go in there again."

A few minutes later, lukewarm vending machine coffees in hand, HB and Keleher had agreed on a game plan. A quick peek into the room before they entered showed Olivia pacing. Their return startled her, and she stopped moving. Her eyes narrowed at HB. "You! You're not police."

She demanded of Shelby, "Why is he here? Does he have information I should know?"

"Have a seat please, Ms. St John-Rivard," said HB. "I'm here as a courtesy to both you and the police. Are you sure you don't want a coffee, water?"

Olivia's jaw tightened. "No! Let's get this over with."

HB didn't hurry as he settled himself opposite Olivia with Shelby at his side, and made a point of enjoying his coffee, which he wasn't. It was awful, but if Olivia could act, so could he.

Undisguised disdain flashed across her face. "I'm not interested in socializing with you. I need to go to the hospital to see my husband and then get to my daughter."

"Here's the thing, see." He stared straight at Olivia. "I was at the hospital earlier when I brought Charlotte to see her father. Curious as to why you keep referring to him as your husband? He was mistreated badly, you know. Another day or two and the outcome might have been a tragedy."

She had the grace to wince, if only for a brief second. "I ... I can't even imagine. Was Charlotte upset?"

"What do you think?" asked Shelby. "Do you even need to ask? Of course she was upset. He nearly died and may have a long road of recovery ahead with life threatening side effects."

"I need to see them, both. Please."

HB tried to work up empathy for the woman but came up short. "Docs are only allowing family and police for now. Sorry."

"But, but ..." she sputtered.

"You are no longer considered family. And Charlotte has stated, quite vehemently, she has no wish to see you. That may change, but for now, she's staying in a safe location, the police are aware of, until Mr. Rivard is well enough to come home." HB watched her deflate, at least for the moment. He needed to get through to her before her armor went up again.

He carried on. "You and I have spoken a few times back at the estate. I was under the impression you were still friends with Xander Michelson or am I mistaken?"

And, she was back. "Friends — *friends*?" she shrieked. "I hope he rots in hell." She plucked tissue from the box beside her. "I left my marriage for him and now look at the mess he's caused. I wouldn't trust him any farther than I could throw him."

Shelby pounced. "What mess exactly are you referring to?"

She and HB stayed silent with the hope of further explanation. But Olivia began to backpedal.

"Why, him coming back here and interfering with the winery is what I mean. I'm sure he's been making plans in the event Etienne wasn't found. I blame him for the alienation between my daughter and me." She fell back against her chair, a smug expression on her face.

HB threw out a casual remark. "You mentioned you left your husband because of Xander - how long was the affair before your now ex-husband learned about it?"

"I'm sure you've done your homework." But she did give them a timeline. HB wondered if there wasn't a tiny bit of pride in the retelling as well.

"As if you don't already know, the affair began when Charlotte was about ten. The divorce happened 2 years after that. Why is this even relevant?"

"Oh, this is just along the lines of general enquiries." HB lowered his voice and leaned forward, as if it were only him and Olivia in the room.

"Were you aware Xander approached my investigation agency *before* the kidnap and wanted my boss to investigate something that hadn't happened yet? Don't you find that more than a little odd? Add that to his behavior over the past few days and the picture has Xander very much involved. Question is - was he working alone? Kevin Butler seems a likely accomplice, but he's dead and not much help to us. That just leaves you, don't you see?"

Olivia's face contorted with rage. "You're the police," she glared at Shelby, deflecting the question. "So investigate. I'm not doing your job for you! You'll find I'm no longer with Xander so how would I even know where to start looking for him." She leaned back and crossed her arms. The sly smile had returned. "However, I wouldn't put it past him to have concocted this whole terrible fiasco and try to implicate me as some sort of revenge for a failed relationship." She glanced between Shelby and HB. "It was all about the money with him. There's your motivation."

"Money?" asked HB. He sensed Shelby ramp up her attention level.

"He was bankrupted by Etienne and because of, um, our relationship, he assumed my family would be good for financial assistance. He assumed wrong."

"I see," said Shelby. "And by you saying that's his motivation, are you implying he is responsible for the kidnapping - to get money? Or am I missing something?"

Olivia pursed her lips. "I think I've said enough. Can I leave now?"

HB deferred the answer to Shelby, who nodded slightly and closed her notebook. "Yes, thank you for your assistance, and you are free to leave. However, we may have more questions, so please don't leave Portland without checking in with us first. Understood?"

It was too good to resist, so HB added. "Yes, Ms. St John-Rivard. Don't leave town."

"Very funny, I'm sure," snarled Olivia.

"Sorry. Couldn't resist. Just a joke." HB wasn't sorry. The woman was a bullseye waiting for darts.

Olivia buttoned up her jacket, smoothed her perfect hair, and left, slamming the door behind her.

As the woman's strident footsteps echoed away from them, HB turned to Shelby and was surprised to see her smiling. He apologized for his last remark. "I know, that was corny, but too good to resist."

"Took the words right out of my mouth. I'll let it pass, this time," she said.

"I'm not telling you how to do your job," said HB, "but I'd think putting a tail on her would be a good idea? She's likely our best bet to lead us to Xander."

"Already in place."

"If you're shorthanded, I can volunteer one of my team," he offered.

"Not this time, I think, but thanks. Unlike you, I need to keep potential legal loopholes airtight. Would hate to see a case dismissed because of a technicality. However, off the record? I can't stop anyone else from following her, but they cannot, I repeat, cannot interfere with authorized police. With the understanding we are all on the same page with new information. Got it?"

"You're the boss. Well, at least in this place. My real boss would likely agree with you though." He looked at the wall clock. "I need to get a move on. Speaking of bosses reminded me I need to check back with Dorothy. And, no offense, but I'm in withdrawal for a decent coffee."

"None taken. Um, before you go, I want to thank you for your help in there. Between us, I think we have her rattled and if she does know where Xander is, or can contact him, she's probably not going to waste any time doing so." They began to walk away from the interview room, and HB started to move ahead to the exit.

"HB? As a way of thanks, maybe we can have lunch or dinner sometime? My treat - you know, on my expense account."

He didn't want to blow this chance to get to know Shelby better and figured the fewer the words the less chance he'd screw it up. "I wouldn't say no."

CHAPTER TWENTY-NINE

"That was a big group, Boss. All the same party?"

Dorothy was helping one of her servers clear the remains of a boisterous retirement party. The partiers had lingered longer than expected, but the tips were worth it. "Reservation for 15, yes. Woman had worked for the same company for twenty-five years. Can you believe it?"

HB snorted. "She'd have been out of jail by now."

Dorothy laughed. "Makes me realize, though, we've been working together for almost as long. Feel ready to retire any time soon?"

"Who me? And then do what? No, long as you want to keep me around, I'll be here."

"Glad to hear it. I hope you're here with some news on the case?"

They moved over to an empty table after HB begged for, and received, a decent cup of coffee. He took a few sips before starting on his report. "You've no idea the swill that passes as coffee I've been forced to drink today."

"All part of my plan to keep you happy in your work. Now, what have you got for me?"

HB recounted the visit to Etienne Rivard at the hospital and then the time spent at the station with the kidnap victim's ex-wife.

Dorothy took it all in. "What's your gut say – do you think she knows where Xander is?"

HB shrugged. "She's an accomplished liar, though I think most of what she says has an element of truth to it. But for some reason, I believed her when she said she doesn't know where he is. Almost a note of panic in her voice, as if she's afraid she's going to be abandoned by him. Totally contradicts what she said about not wanting to see him or caring about him. Maybe we need to give out Quail awards for some of these clients."

Dorothy raised an eyebrow. "Seems you spending time with Sergeant Keleher has brought out your sense of humor. Will this be a good thing?"

He focused on finishing his coffee, but Dorothy thought she'd struck a nerve. He was interested in Shelby. She let up on the teasing. "Award or not, do you think she's a flight risk?"

"The police have a tail on her, and unofficially Jordan's doing the same. He texted me just before I came in here to say since Olivia arrived back at the winery, she's staying put."

Dorothy nodded. "Good to have extra eyes on her. And I expect the police to be monitoring her phone, but I doubt she's stupid enough to try and contact Xander. Wonder where that boy disappeared to?"

"I have an idea about that, boss. But first, how's Charlotte? I left a message with Max, but he hasn't returned my call yet."

Dorothy smiled. "Dad seems to be enjoying her company. He took advantage of Olivia being at the station and took Charlotte back to the house to pick up some clothes and her school things."

"So, you and Max are okay with her staying a while longer?"

"Until this case is settled, or her father can take care of her, it's not a problem. I believe Alanna would love to impart some tips on her dress code and appearance, but Charlotte is already her own person ..."

"Is she ever. Not sure how bent she might be on the P.I. thing, but you never know."

"And you, HB, will get the credit for it if she does. Well done. Now, you said you might have an idea about where Xander is?"

"It's just a hunch, boss. But I wondered if you might want to tag along first thing in the morning?"

***

The sun had been up less than an hour when Dorothy and HB parked outside Knockdown Warriors. She enjoyed the early morning drive in her Jeep, no matter what the reason. Plus they'd agreed her vehicle wouldn't be recognized by Xander if he was in the area.

"So, this is where you work out the frustrations of work?" she teased.

The boxing club wasn't in the best part of the city and the façade had seen better days. Dirty windows were adorned with posters and flyers – many long out of date. A trash can overflowed near the front door, but lights were on even at this early hour.

"After you, Boss. I'll introduce you to a friend who owns the place."

He pushed open the door and allowed her to enter ahead of him. It was the smell she reacted to first as she gulped back the first breath. Gross. Reminiscent of high school gym classes, but much more pungent. She heard the slap and thump of someone working a punching bag. Two fight rings took up most of the center space, a skipping rope draped over one, and towels on the other. Two youths, she judged about nineteen or twenty, hopped up and over the ropes. Sporting headgear and bright red gloves, they were ready to exercise. She'd stick to running.

"This way, boss."

She followed him to a door which looked as if it had doubled as a punching bag more than once. The name Amos Agnew – Proprietor was faded. Not too much of any profits went into maintenance, she surmised.

HB rapped on the door, and a gruff voice bid them enter. Behind an old metal desk sat a grizzled man of about 60. Intense blue eyes sat beneath the bushiest pair of eyebrows Dorothy had ever seen. The stern face crinkled into a smile at the sight of HB.

"Holden, my man. This is a surprise. And who's your young friend? I didn't know you were recruiting new members?"

Dorothy recognized a charmer when she heard one. She suspected Amos Agnew might be cut from similar cloth as her dad, which made her instantly like him. Not too many called HB by his full name, so the character must be someone special in HB's books.

"Amos, this is my boss, Dorothy Dennehy."

Amos stood to shake her hand. "Aha, so I finally get to meet the famous 'boss'. Holden here has been known to sing your praises from time to time. I take it this might not be a social type visit?"

"Mind if I close the door?" asked HB.

"Sure. Take a seat if you like. I'd offer coffee or something stronger, but the coffee maker's on the fritz, and I suppose it is a bit early for the other. So, what can I do you for?" Amos looked at her, but this was HB's arena, literally.

"HB asked me to come along in regard to a case we're working, so I'll let him explain."

No preamble; HB cut straight to the heart of the visit. "Stonefist Sandy, Amos. Has he been around lately, like in the last day or two?"

Amos rubbed arthritic knuckles below his chin. "Let me think." He turned to check a clipboard hanging behind him. "Right, last week. He was in late and stayed till closing time. And he was angry when he left."

"Angry about what," asked Dorothy.

"Tried to blame it on me. He was in a hurry to leave, and we were closing, see. He tore one of his gloves on the edge of his locker. You know, the inside of the door where it's sharp. Said he had a good mind to charge me for a new pair because I don't keep the place in good repair." Amos lifted both hands as he shrugged. "Is he in some kind of trouble?"

"Some kind, yeah, you could say that. Long story short, we're anxious to find him and talk to him about a kidnapping and he seems to have disappeared. I, uh, wondered if we might poke around in the back rooms." He turned to Dorothy. "Some of the regular, trusted, members have a key to this place so they can come in during off hours."

"And you're thinking Stonefist might have squirreled himself away in one of my back rooms? Do the police know you're on his trail here?"

"I'd rather play out my hunch first. If anything turns up, for sure we'll let the cops know," explained HB.

"I see," said Amos. "Then go ahead. If you find anything, let me know."

"Thank you, Mr. Agnew," said Dorothy as they made to leave his office.

"Call me Amos. Any friend of Holden's, well you know. Good luck."

Dorothy followed HB as he headed toward a corridor away from the main gym, where she eyed the boxing rings again. "Question."

HB stopped. "Sure, Boss, what?"

She pointed at the rings. "Why, if they are square, are they called rings?"

He explained. "Some say because back in the day when people fought on the street, spectators gathered in a circle around them. And I think there's some kind of rule from around 1700 when boxers or fighters met to duke it out, they started their positions in a small center circle area."

"Like a face off in hockey?"

"Kinda, yeah."

"I see. Okay, thanks." Interesting trivia to file away, and she indicated to him to lead on.

They passed a locker room and showers. Dorothy noted facilities were available for women as well, but she could never see herself in such a male-dominated space. Testosterone coated the walls like a layer of paint.

They poked their heads into a couple of empty changing rooms and a janitor's cubby. Near the back exit was another door. Equipment Storage said the door's sign.

"Last chance," sighed HB as he opened the door. He found a light switch. Barbells and weights littered the area. A treadmill that had seen better days now doubled as a drying rack.

But wait. "HB, look," Dorothy pointed to the treadmill. "Whose gym clothes?"

They moved in for a closer look. A fleece-lined hoodie, showing a label from an upscale sporting goods store, sat atop a pair of well-used track pants.

"Boss, over here."

Dorothy saw a rumpled sleeping bag and paper coffee cups on the floor. Next to an empty Michard Estates Winery bottle.

"Bingo!" exclaimed HB.

"Well played, HB! Let's not touch anything. I'll call Shelby and she can get a team over here to check for any evidence to link this to Xander, and you call Jordan. Have him keep an eye on this exit — from a distance — in case Xander returns. He could be faster getting here than the police."

Then they informed Amos of their find and that the police were on their way. "I'm sorry if it will be a disruption to your day," said Dorothy. "Can't be helped."

"So Stonefist Sandy, eh? Bugger. Guess I'll need to cancel his membership" He barked a short laugh. "I can turn members away from the entrance if you like. Should I ask anyone here to leave?"

Dorothy nodded. "Turning people away is good, but anyone here should stay until the police have come and talked to them ..."

She was interrupted when a sweating gym member burst into the office. "Amos! My locker has been tampered with and my gun is missing!"

***

Three hours later, Dorothy and HB were still at the gym. Forensics combed the makeshift hideaway, filling several plastic evidence bags.

Marcus Freeman, whose gun was stolen, had been interviewed at length by detectives. He had a license for the Smith and Wesson handgun he used for target practice and had forgotten to take it home the previous day. His locker was now covered in fingerprint powder.

Amos provided whatever information he had on Xander Michelson, which wasn't much. Last known address was the apartment above the laundromat – no surprise.

Once the detectives had received verbal confirmation from Shelby Keleher that HB and Dorothy were legitimately involved with the investigation, they were allowed to leave. Outside again on the sidewalk, Dorothy took a couple of deep breaths.

"Don't know how you guys can breathe the air in there," she laughed. "I bet Shelby is miffed she was tied up in an administrative review and couldn't be here. I'll try and touch base with her later to see what shakes loose from materials recovered. Unless," she looked at HB, "you'd rather call her?"

HB cleared his throat. "Sure. Can do. But seeing as we're free to go now, I'd also like to check in with Charlotte and get an update on her father. It's nearly noon and she likely wants to get back to the hospital."

"Do you want me to ask my dad if he'll take her?" said Dorothy. "You know he'd be glad to."

"Right, but I'm kind of invested in her, you know?"

"Got it. And I need to show up at the bar and explain to the staff why I'm late for work!"

"Yeah, sorry. I had no idea we'd be here this long."

"Wouldn't have missed it," she said as they reached her Jeep and got in. She started the engine and pulled away from the curb. "I have an idea. The police will be busy today on the hunt for Xander, Etienne is recovering in hospital, and Olivia seems to be staying put. I say we deserve a break. Dinner at my house this evening? I'll ask Rolin as well. Good chance to get everyone caught up all at once. And no, you don't have to bring anything. Just be there for 6, okay?"

"You're the boss, so what can I say?" joked HB.

Dorothy smiled, and hoped her dad would be up to putting on one of his famous meals on short notice!

CHAPTER THIRTY

Dorothy opened her front door to see Rolin and HB. "Punctual as always, gentlemen. Come in. I'm busy in the kitchen, so you know where to hang your coats and then come on through." She hurried back to the heart of her home.

"Something smells good, doesn't it, Rolin?" said HB as he put his coat away. And then he made a face.

Rolin smiled. "I know what you're thinking - be nice. And you're not one to talk, are you? What Dorothy lacks in culinary skills she makes up for in other areas. That being said, I'm certain the aromas coming from the kitchen will be a result of Max's kitchen creations and not his daughter's."

"And that's why you're a lawyer and I'm not," laughed HB. "You know how to cover all the bases. Anyway, wonder what he's drummed up for us tonight?"

"Take a seat you two," instructed Dorothy when they entered the kitchen. Alanna patted the seat next to her for Rolin, who soon had her smiling with his genuine interest in her day.

Charlotte's face lit up when she spied HB. "Sit next to me, HB."

When everyone was seated, Dorothy held up a hand. "Before we start, there's one rule. No shop talk until we've finished eating. I don't want anything to spoil the amazing meal Dad's gone to a lot of trouble for. Got it?"

"Thanks, darlin'. I believe mealtime is to count as down time for you hard working folk."

"Cheers to that," toasted HB, raising his glass.

Dorothy added to the toast, "And to you, Dad, for another hearty meal - perfect for this time of year." She waved her hand across the table and its array of platters and bowls of appetizing fare. "Tuck in, everyone."

Dorothy recognized the smile on her father's face. She knew how much he enjoyed cooking. with his preference for the old traditional Irish recipes - many handed down to him. To cook for a crowd was icing on the cake.

Tonight's specialty was well received, judging by exclamations of approval around the table. Alanna smiled at her husband; Dorothy appreciated her quiet, but loving, show of support for him.

To Dorothy's surprise, Charlotte appeared to enjoy the meal. She'd been afraid her father's Colcannon with pork sausages wouldn't appeal to her. By now, Dorothy had learned Charlotte never sugar-coated anything and if she hadn't liked the dish, all would have known about it.

The teenager had nearly cleaned her plate when she turned to ask Max about the dish.

"So, what is in this whatever you call it, Col something. It's really yummy. I think my dad would like it, too."

Max loved a compliment and beamed at her. "Well, lass, I could tell you it's a secret recipe, or you could look it up on Google with that device you always have in your hand. Long and short of it - it's called Colcannon and is made with mashed potatoes and cabbage, plus a few of my secret spices." He reached for the serving dish. "Would you like some more, then? And don't forget to have another slice or two of Aunt Alanna's soda bread. She's a master at making it."

Charlotte's nose wrinkled at the mention of cabbage. "Ewww, cabbage... but it tastes so good. Yes, I'll have some more, thank you."

HB and Rolin followed suit and piled their plates. Conversation was kept to a minimum as they all enjoyed the repast. And then it was Alanna's turn to shine as she brought out dessert, to a round of oohs as she placed her special raspberry torte on the table. Fresh brewed coffee was the finishing touch.

When all agreed they could eat no more, Dorothy suggested they move to the living room.

Charlotte arranged herself between her surrogate parents. She focused on her phone and seemed to tune out the conversation around her. Earlier she'd tried to interest Dorothy in a strategy game she liked to play. Dorothy found a diplomatic way to say it wasn't her thing, but it was obvious Charlotte could become engrossed in the activity. Especially now she knew her father was alive, her anger had dimmed significantly, so Dorothy figured the game would be a good diversion while they talked.

Max leaned back comfortably into the corner of the sofa, but to Dorothy's eye he looked tired. She hoped he hadn't overdone it with the meal.

"... no offense, Charlotte, but your mother is not a nice person."

Dorothy had lost the thread of the conversation but snapped back to it when Charlotte responded to HB's observation. He must have been talking about the joint interview he'd participated in with Shelby Keleher. She'd get the details from his write-up later.

Charlotte looked up from her phone, face pinched in the scowl Dorothy was now familiar with. "I haven't changed my mind, you know. I hate her. She left once and she can go again, for good. And they'd better catch Uncle Xander and put him in jail, too."

Max reached over and tousled the top of her head. "Darlin' you need to let that anger go, it only hurts you, not them."

"Whatever."

Dorothy could empathize with her disgust, but knew she wanted to talk more about Xander with Rolin, and the kidnapper's flight from the law. Probably better if Charlotte was elsewhere. A diversion was called for.

"I need volunteers for kitchen duty. Any takers?"

HB was first to jump in. "I'll do my share. How about you, Charlotte? We could see if there's any of that mashed potato dish for me to take home. Coming?"

Dorothy smiled at her friend. He'd picked up on what was needed, and she'd thank him later.

Charlotte wore an aggrieved expression on her face at having to shut off her phone. She sighed deeply and stood. The miserable look faded as she egged on HB. "Catch me if you can, HB. I'll get to the potatoes before you!" HB stretched and cracked his knuckles. "We'll see about that." And with a nod to the room, they both disappeared into the kitchen.

Then Max lumbered to his feet and stretched his hand out to Alanna. "I think we'll make tracks for home darlin'. Alanna and I are getting on you know, and after toiling in the kitchen for my favorite daughter and her friends, we're ready to call it a day. Hope you don't mind."

Alanna swatted playfully at Max. "Speak for yourself. I'm ready to dance the night away. But I think this old man wants to watch his favorite show on television. He's hooked on ...guess what? *Criminal Minds*."

Dorothy smiled indulgently. "Oh Dad, haven't you had enough criminals to deal with in real life?"

"I like to solve the cases before they do. You and HB have a good handle on this one, so you don't need my input. And it's heartwarming to see him take such an interest in the young lass." A twinkle came to his eye. "So much fun to have a young person about. Reminds me of you at this age. Sassy as all get out."

"Don't you dare laugh, Rolin. I have no idea what my father means. Me? Sassy? Hah!"

Max laughed, but didn't say another word, and let Alanna lead him back to the connecting door leading to their own apartment. She called over her shoulder as they left. "If this old man falls asleep, Dorothy, I'll still be awake for Charlotte when it's time to send her over. Good night."

"Another excellent meal, Dee. Max outdid himself - he impressed a teenager," said Rolin.

"I think it's done him good to have Charlotte stay with them for a while. Not sure how much longer, though. Guess it will depend on her father's recovery. But in any event, I have a feeling they've become lifelong friends, so it would be nice for them to stay in touch when this is all over."

Giggles and the clink and clatter of dishes came from the kitchen. "And HB is taken with her as well, it seems," said Rolin.

Dorothy laughed. "For all her rough edges, she knows how to wrap the men around her little finger. When it suits her."

"Ah, I see you're not fooled by her ways?"

Dorothy shook her head. "Sorry, that didn't come out the way I intended. You know me, not much experience with kids, of any age. She has a lot of growing up to do, but I do see glimpses of a smart young woman on the horizon."

She sat next to him on the sofa and tried to stifle a yawn. "It's not the company, really. I'll be glad when this case is resolved. In other words, the sooner Xander is apprehended the better for all concerned. I hope the next 24 hours will see him caught. HB has Jordan following some leads as well. Even if I don't get a cent for the bill he's run up with me, it will be good to close the file on this one."

"I'm sure there'll be a way to recover your fees. If need be, leave it with me."

Another yawn overtook her, this time in earnest. "I am sorry Rolin, but I'm beat and I'm afraid I'll have to call it a night. Do you mind?"

Rolin stood. "Of course not. On one condition. We have a proper dinner when this is over. A dinner for just the two of us."

"Agreed. And, yes, I like the sound of that. Now, I take it you and HB drove here separately; it sounds like he and Charlotte aren't quite done. I may have to kick them both out."

"Yes, I don't need to wait for him. Unless you want me to give him a push?"

She smiled. "I'll have them on their way shortly, trust me. Thanks for being part of dinner this evening."

"Anytime, although I seemed not to have contributed much. See you in the morning for a run before we start our day?"

"That's the plan," she said as she saw him to the door.

She watched him drive away, then walked back toward the kitchen, and paused outside the doorway. Charlotte was speaking softly, her words rooted Dorothy to the spot.

"So, HB. That lawyer guy, Rolin? I watched him at dinner. I think he likes — I mean *likes* — Dorothy. Did you know that? And she tries to pretend not to see it, but I'd say she knows and likes him too."

"I don't disagree with you, Charlotte. But Dorothy and Rolin are adults and don't need you pointing out the obvious, to either of them."

"All I'm saying is, they're like, old, you know? Do people their age get stupid with romance stuff?"

Dorothy was glad she was hidden from view. How could a 14-year-old make her feel like an awkward teenager? She couldn't hear HB's mumbled response and decided it was time to stop the discussion.

"Dishes all done?" she asked brightly as she entered the room. And yes, the kitchen was clean and tidy. A couple of take away containers held leftovers for HB.

"We're all done, Boss. And I guess I'll be on my way. Time Charlotte, here, was in bed."

"Thanks for helping, you two. And now, Charlotte, yes, you need to get on the other side of that door. Alanna is waiting up for you. Goodnight."

"Nite, Dorothy. And bye for now, HB. See you soon."

Doors opened and closed. Ah, peace and quiet at last. Dorothy pulled out a kitchen chair and sat. Playing over in her mind what she'd overheard. She tied it in with gratitude for both HB and Rolin. Two very different men, but equally important to her. She had relied on both at different times, especially in times of personal crisis. HB was a steadfast and loyal friend. Rolin was ...

Just what was Rolin to her? A friend, of course. A business partner, and ... Don't go there! She abruptly stood and pushed thoughts she wasn't ready to acknowledge off to the side. But she had a feeling she wouldn't be able to ignore those thoughts much longer.

She turned out the lights and made her way upstairs to bed. She drifted off, only to dream of finding a treasure chest wrapped in chains belonging to the anchor of the *Aye*. Single-handedly she pulled the slippery chain up from watery depths and got the chest on board. She had an overpowering need to get it open and smashed a jar of chocolate covered almonds against it until the lock shattered. With great effort she pushed up on the lid and saw ...Rolin.

CHAPTER THIRTY-ONE

"The colors are good this year," commented Dorothy as she and HB drove into Portland for a mid-morning update with Shelby Keleher. Most trees in the area showed signs of autumn's advance. The air was cool, the sky a cloudless blue.

"If you say so, Boss."

"Maybe more so along the waterfront. Rolin and I went for a quick run this morning. Definitely more than a hint of colder temperatures in the air. In a month it will be Thanksgiving. Can you believe it?"

"Makes me wonder who Charlotte will be celebrating the holidays with," mused HB.

She was ready with an answer. "Not to worry. If she's not settled back with her father by then, she's more than welcome to spend it right where she is now. Make you feel better?" She couldn't resist a tease. "Maybe I'll invite Shelby Keleher to join us as well — if she has no other plans. How's that?"

HB twisted in the seat beside her, ignored her question and focused on sipping coffee from the travel mug he'd brought with him. "Wonder what kind of update we're going to get. Weird she wouldn't tell us over the phone."

Dorothy expected she knew the reason. It would be an excuse for Shelby to see HB. But that was men for you, didn't always see the obvious where romance might be involved. She'd drop the teasing for now, bound to be more opportunities on the horizon. She parked at the police station. "Guess we're about to find out."

On their way to Keleher's office, they passed Jake Warner's desk. HB nodded at him, and Jake grunted a good morning in return. "Leg any better?" asked HB.

"Slow going is an understatement. More physio today. Time will tell. On your way to see her?" He tipped his head in the direction of his superior's office.

"We are. She has an update on the Rivard kidnapping. You haven't heard anything on locating Michelson, have you?"

"Not for lack of effort, from what I hear. She'll have the latest. And, you've been spotted."

Dorothy moved ahead, with HB behind, and into Shelby's office.

"Have a seat." Her all-business tone set the mood. No small talk.

"Any news on Michelson?" asked Dorothy.

"Nothing so far. We found his passport, so he can't leave the country. Although you and I both know with a little effort he could slip into Canada without it."

"I'd rather he slipped into a jail cell," remarked HB.

Dorothy noticed Shelby conceded a slight smile in his direction.

"We will get him. And let me thank you again, HB, for the lead on the missing gun. Hunches don't always pay off, but this time it did." Shelby referred to a file on her desk. "As to Michelson's location - we've had numerous calls coming in about possible sightings, so we have every reason to believe he's still in the area. And armed. Bank and credit card accounts have been frozen. Although we're certain he had a sizable amount of cash on hand, losing the ransom money will hurt."

"He must have been harboring a grudge against Etienne Rivard for a long time. But what he ever saw in Etienne's ex-wife I'll never understand," said Dorothy.

"I'll second that, Boss."

"So, what do you have for us, Shelby?" asked Dorothy.

"We executed a search warrant on the buildings and property located at Michard Estates Winery first thing this morning. Ms. St John-Rivard was not amused to put it lightly. I've still got officers there checking the fields — don't expect anything will surface but need to be sure. Here's what we did find of interest."

Shelby reached behind for a bulky plastic evidence bag and placed it on her desk.

HB whistled. "Wow, are those Hayabusa?"

Shelby pushed the bag over to HB who peered through the plastic to have a better look at the red boxing gloves. "You're familiar, I take it?"

"Only second hand. I could never afford these. Last I checked they start at $300.00 a pair. They belong to Xander, then? And found at the house. Interesting."

Dorothy noted. "Maybe because they're so expensive he didn't want to risk keeping them at the gym."

"We think there's another reason," said Shelby. "Based on two things. We found them hidden under Charlotte's bed and take a closer look. Knuckle side."

Dorothy peered closely and spied the tear in the leather material right away. "A small piece missing, about the same size found on Frisco Butler's body?"

Beside her, HB had tensed. "I better not be the one who finds this guy. Hiding evidence of his crime under Charlotte's bed. Damn coward!" He looked at Shelby. "Charlotte doesn't need to know, does she? She has a hate on for her mother and Xander — this won't help."

"I see no reason for her to find out. But there's more. Do you see the blood?"

"You've got him now. It's Butler's blood?" HB's voice held a note of victory.

"Being analyzed as we speak."

Dorothy handed the bag back to Shelby. "Did the search turn up anything else of use?"

Shelby wore a Cheshire cat smile. "Indeed, we did. A burner phone. Most calls to another burner, but a couple of calls made to ... Oh, go on, take a guess."

"I'd assume one burner might be in Olivia's possession?" said Dorothy. "But no idea on the other. You have an idea, HB?"

He shook his head. Dorothy sensed Shelby enjoyed playing out the information reveal. For HB's benefit? Trying to impress him? Maybe. She waited.

"The St John family home, in New York."

Shelby's phone rang. "I have to take this. One second."

Dorothy turned to HB and lowered her voice. "Still not a lot of direct evidence linking Olivia to all of this. Those phone calls suggest they'd been back in touch before she arrived back in Portland. Maybe she's smarter than we give her credit for and made sure nothing would turn up at the house to implicate her."

"Other than phone calls, there probably isn't any physical evidence, Boss. Feels like she knows how to hedge all her bets to keep the dirt from landing on her."

Dorothy hoped if Charlotte inherited her mother's abilities, she'd use them in non-criminal ways. More reason to try and steer her in the right direction. But not her concern. HB on the other hand?

"Apologies," said Keleher as she hung up her desk phone. "That was to inform me Ms. St. John has retained a very pricey criminal lawyer, and she is not to talk with us in future without her present."

"Nothing says guilty like lawyering up," commented HB. "Who's the lawyer?"

"Alexandra Drakos."

"Pricey. I've a friend who knows her." Dorothy considered the update. "The lawyer wouldn't want her talking with any police officials, but would that include me, or HB?"

"Oh, what a shame. I didn't think to ask for clarification," said Shelby.

"Good one, Boss," teased HB. "Sure you two aren't related somehow? "

"Irish genes," said Dorothy, and Shelby, at the same time, followed by laughter.

Dorothy noted the outburst had been loud enough to attract attention from desks closest to Shelby's office, and immediate return to serious mode.

"I'll let you know what the lab says about the blood, but I would be very surprised if it's not Frisco Butler's."

"Shelby, what's your theory on what happened to him, unless you want to keep that quiet for now? This will only be between us three." And maybe Rolin if need be.

Shelby sighed. "It's all supposition until we can talk with Xander of course. On the surface it would seem Michelson and Butler were partnered in this extortion attempt. There is evidence to suggest Michelson had befriended Butler a while ago ..."

"That would have to have been after Michelson left the winery. Which was more than 2 years ago I believe." Dorothy pulled out her notebook and referred to information previously gathered. "Yes, the bankruptcy was almost 2 and a half years ago and Michelson, apparently, went off grid shortly after."

"Right," continued Shelby. "Butler was a petty drug dealer. Drifted into our area about three years ago. We're working his contacts to see if we can pin down when he and Michelson first crossed paths."

"But why was he killed?" asked HB. "That's the question. Although having seen the nastier side of Michelson, I'd say Michelson decided not to share the ransom."

"It may have been an accident," said Shelby. "Think about it. The ransom money wasn't yet in play and Michelson could have used an extra pair of hands keeping an eye on Rivard."

"That's one angle and sounds plausible. But I'm not sure. Michelson is crafty. Don't forget he came to seek my agency services before this crime happened. A set up if ever there was one — framing Butler knowing he'd be dead?"

"I think I'll use a Rubik's Cube as the icon for these files," said Shelby. She stood. "Sorry, I need to be elsewhere, but thanks for the brainstorming. Maybe next time we can meet at your bar, Dorothy. I hear the food and service is top drawer."

"Anytime," agreed Dorothy. She and HB took their leave as Shelby confirmed she'd be in touch with any new information.

Back in Dorothy's Jeep, they reviewed what they'd learned with Shelby.

"Not sure if there's any value in contacting Olivia right now. I bet she'll be expecting us to try, so that in itself might throw her off a bit," said HB.

"Agreed. Our resources would be better spent tracking down Michelson."

HB's phone buzzed. "It's Charlotte."

Dorothy focused on driving as HB spoke with her new houseguest. It was a short call and he disconnected.

"Do you mind if I take Charlotte back to the hospital to see her father? If we consider it part of the investigation as well, I might pick up some useful information regarding Butler?"

"HB," laughed Dorothy. "You don't need to ask. I'll drop you at your car. But don't forget …"

"Yes, I know. A full report."

CHAPTER THIRTY-TWO

HB picked up Charlotte just before 1:00. She raced down the front steps as he pulled into Dorothy's driveway and hopped in the car.

"Let's go already. I thought you were going to be here an hour ago."

HB put the car in park and turned to look at her. "And hello to you as well. How are you?" He threw as much sarcasm as he could into his greeting. They were not getting off to a good start and she needed a course correction. She could pull this crap with her mother, but it wasn't on with him.

"What?" Charlotte finished buckling her seat belt and then paid attention to her companion. "I'm late to see my dad."

HB took a breath. "Look at me. I am not your mother, or your enemy. In fact, I didn't have to come and get you. Buses run from here to the hospital, you know." Then he felt he might have overstepped, but what the heck.

She blinked a few times and her eyes glistened. "I ... I'm sorry. You're right." She bit on a nail. "We're still friends?"

HB grunted, put the car in drive and they headed toward the hospital. He wouldn't let her off so easily.

They drove in silence for a few minutes, until Charlotte broke the ice. "Are we nearly there yet? I'm so anxious to see my dad. Maybe he'll be able to talk more with me today than the last time." She paused, as if HB's recent words made her think. "Um, you must want to ask him questions, too. Right? I guess we both want answers, but he may not have what either of us need."

He couldn't stay upset with her, and it seemed like she was offering an olive branch. Good thing because he didn't like being at odds with anyone he cared about. "Hey, listen to you. You're starting to think like a P.I. already." He'd hit the mark when he saw her smile. "Let's play it by ear and see how he is today. Sergeant Keleher's also anxious to find out more so they can anticipate Xander's next move. I know you said you didn't have any idea, but sometimes your brain can make connections when you're not trying so hard." They'd reached the hospital, and he parked the car. "By chance do you have any new thoughts about where Xander might be?"

As they left the car, Charlotte turned to HB and said, "I know I told you I have no idea but...I might have remembered someone."

She had his full attention, and he didn't interrupt, letting her talk as they continued their way to her father's room.

"I remember he mentioned a friend who stays at a marina — you know, like the one your boss works at? Uncle Xander once promised he'd take me there for sailing lessons ... Anyway, he said his friend, Steve, docks a boat there. They might be friends from university or something. But we never did it. Do you think he might be there?"

HB came to a full stop. "Charlotte, you're a genius. I'd better let Shelby know about this. I don't suppose you have a last name? Or anything else about him?"

She shrugged. "Sorry, no. Now can I go see my dad?"

He tapped numbers on his phone. "Hold on while I talk to the sergeant - this is important."

HB spoke with Shelby, relaying what Charlotte had told him. He hung up, smiling.

"Ok, let's go visit your dad. The sergeant will try and meet up with us later."

***

After a quick check with nursing staff, and a nod to the officer stationed outside Rivard's room, HB softly opened the door. Charlotte moved ahead of him. Monitors still beeped, but there weren't as many IV bags hanging as last time. That should be a good sign.

Even better, Etienne Rivard was awake, smiling at the sight of his daughter, who was ready to sprint to his side. HB held her back for a moment. "Don't crush him, he needs to breathe."

HB had questions, but the bonding time between Charlotte and her dad was more important. He tried to remain unobtrusive as Charlotte made sure her dad was going to recover. Etienne's voice was raspy and weak as he questioned Charlotte about school and living arrangements. They talked for a few more minutes, until Rivard needed a break.

Charlotte looked at HB and whispered. "He looks better, doesn't he?"

HB nodded. Truthfully, he agreed. The last 24 hours had seen an improvement which should help Charlotte worry less.

"Oh, sorry. I drifted off a bit. Who's your friend, Charlotte?"

HB stepped forward. "It's good to see you awake, Mr. Rivard. I met you the other day, but you were in rough shape and likely don't remember. My name is Holden Bartholomew. A private investigator with Quail Investigations. We're working with the police on your case. Specifically trying to locate

Xander Michelson. Do you feel up to answering a few questions for me?"

Etienne croaked out a reply he would try his best. He couldn't take his eyes off his daughter and they held hands as Charlotte sat on the side of the bed.

Charlotte chipped in to say, "You can call him HB. I'm sure he won't mind. I have so much to tell you, Daddy, but this is the man who rescued me from Uncle Xander. I'll never call him uncle again."

Etienne's face scowled, and the blood pressure monitor beeps increased. "Rescued you? What happened? If he hurt you ..." Exhausted, he fell back and closed his eyes, but managed to mutter. "I've done a lot of thinking about him while I lie here. I had my suspicions ... What can I do to help catch him?"

HB lowered his voice for Charlotte. "He sounds pooched. I think we might have to cut this short. The doctor wouldn't be happy if we overtire him and delay his recovery. If there's any more talk, maybe it should be on happier things."

"Got it," she said, as a small moan came from her father's bed.

Etienne managed to smile and mouthed a thank you to HB. Charlotte proceeded to tell him about staying with Max and Alanna. "They're the best people and I like it there but it's just until you can come home."

"Um, Charlotte, I think your dad needs a break, and I'm dying for a coffee. Would you mind getting some from the machine in the lobby? You can get a cold drink." He opened his wallet for a few bills. "Here take this. I'll bring your dad up to date with the investigation before a nurse throws us out."

"I'd rather stay here," she complained. HB gave her a look and he knew she understood when she said. "But I know he's getting tired. I'll be right back." She grabbed the money and left. The monitor's beeps had returned to normal.

"You have quite the daughter, Mr. Rivard. She's been so worried about you and wouldn't let me rest until you were found. You have a lot to be proud of."

"I was so afraid I'd never see her again." He took a breath and strengthened his voice. "I assume you want to talk without her around."

"Yes. Our priority, and the police, is to find Xander. He's a loose cannon right now and the sooner we get him the better. Charlotte mentioned a friend of Xander's, Steve somebody, who might have a boat docked in the area. Ring any bells? Like a last name, or where the actual location might be? I can pass that on to Sergeant Keleher."

"Keleher, yes. She's been here a lot." Etienne's eyes were closed but he muttered, "Steve Kinney. All three of us were at the same university. I was friends with both, but I never knew he and Xander were friends. Nice guy."

"Thanks, I'll pass this along to the cops. Sergeant Keleher will likely be along later and will confirm this information with you. You should get some more rest. I can bring Charlotte back again tomorrow, or sooner if we get any good news."

Charlotte returned, creeping into the room with HB's coffee and a drink for herself. She spoke in an exaggerated whisper, thinking her dad asleep. "I met the sergeant in the lobby, and she wants to meet with us before she comes to see Dad."

HB nodded. "We'd better go then. Say bye to your dad, for now."

"I'll see you again tomorrow, Dad." She laid a kiss on his forehead, and a solitary tear landed on his cheek. She swiped at her face as she rushed out the door.

Tears. Right up there with hospitals as things HB tried to avoid. He made no reference to her distress as he steered her to the lobby where Shelby waited for them. By then the tears were history, replaced with a Charlotte-sized rant.

She angrily tossed her empty drink container in a nearby trash can. "I don't understand why adults do these things. Like, Uncle Xander. Why kidnap my dad? I know it's all mixed up with my mother but there has to be something else — not just money. He always said I was his special girl and ..."

He wondered if Charlotte had spotted Shelby, who stood to one side, a bemused expression lighting her face. Fortunately there was no one else in the area to witness his attempt at parenting.

"Charlotte, you'll learn as you get older that adults are complicated. I bet by the time we find him, he'll have a barrel-full of explanations, or excuses."

Charlotte started to laugh. "You know what you just said?"

HB shook his head.

"You said a *barrel-full*, you know, the winery. You made a pun!"

"Mr. Bartholomew is full of untapped talents," said Shelby as she moved toward them.

Great, he was outnumbered now. Especially when Charlotte moved in for the kill and turned his words back on him. "Are you complicated HB?"

He cleared his throat, conscious of Shelby's presence. "Um, a discussion for another day."

"Charlotte, he's right. Adults are complicated. We should probably leave it at that. Or am I wrong, Mr. Bartholomew?"

HB locked eyes with Shelby and momentarily lost his train of thought. "Er, sure. Listen, that Steve Kinney I told you about — they were all at university together. Although, Etienne wasn't aware of Xanders friendship with him."

Keleher grew serious. "A good lead we're following up on, thanks. How is your dad today - think he's up for some questions, Charlotte?" Charlotte seemed pleased to be the one asked for advice about her father and HB gave Shelby marks for treating her as an adult.

"He's tired. We talked to him for a bit, but he keeps falling asleep. He was upset when he found out about Xander trying to hurt me, and HB coming to my rescue."

"I understand, thanks. I'll keep it in mind, and I promise I won't stay too long. After I check in with him, I'll check for updates on Mr. Kinney's location." Shelby led HB aside a couple of steps from Charlotte. "What's your opinion, do you think Rivard's up to questions?"

They discussed Rivard's condition and the case in general, when HB noticed Charlotte's attention had begun to wander. She showed signs of restlessness once the spotlight was focused away from her. She'd opened her phone, engrossed in its contents again.

HB rattled his car keys. "Charlotte, why don't you go wait in the car. I'll be along in a few minutes. You and your game should be happy together until then?"

Wordlessly, Charlotte snatched the keys and was gone even as HB's advice to lock the door faded away.

"Shelby. Before you head upstairs, are there any updates on the stolen gun? Or do we assume Michelson has it, and when we find one, we find the other? I hate the idea of this guy being on the loose with one."

"Your assumption is shared by the department, and I agree Michelson is more than dangerous now. An updated BOLO regarding Michelson has gone out to include the gun's description. According to its owner, he believes the magazine isn't full, but could still hold 6 rounds." She pulled out her phone. "Here, I'll send you a copy you can pass on to Dorothy. Off the record, for now, I appreciate the assistance you've both provided. My past experience with cop-turned-p.i. hasn't always been good. Dorothy is an exception.

"In my books, when you work with Dorothy, you get the best."

Shelby laughed. "A tiny bit biased, I think. We'll talk more later." She moved toward the elevator, pressed the button, and turned back to him with a smile. "Now I know you're a boxer, I may have to come and watch you spar some time."

Left momentarily speechless by her remark, he found his voice, ignored her comment, and responded, "I'm taking Charlotte home now. You can text me with any updates."

She stepped into the elevator. "The only update I want is that we've found him, and the gun."

He couldn't agree more as she was swallowed up behind the closing door.

CHAPTER THIRTY-THREE

"I think I should go home with you, Boss. Xander is out there somewhere and who knows what his frame of mind is. He's been aggravated with you since day one. You know how that kind of thing can grow ugly fast."

Dorothy had grabbed her jacket and keys, ready to head home for a quick shower to freshen up for the evening rush. Thursdays were becoming as busy as a Friday or Saturday night.

"He's either gone to ground or long gone by now, HB. I'll be fine. If you want to keep busy, an extra pair of hands in the kitchen would be welcome."

"I'll pass. Guess I'll tackle paperwork – only this much more enjoyable than dish washing," HB held up a pinched thumb and finger. "Just keep an eye out, okay."

"I will. Right, I need to go so I can be back here in an hour."

The afternoon had turned warm, and Dorothy drove with windows down, her mind running between the case, the dinner rush, and thoughts of Rolin. The latter had intruded more and more over the last couple of days. She'd picked up on the vibes from Paul almost from their first contact. But Rolin – it was complicated and while her defenses against another man in her life were weakening, she didn't know if she was ready. Or ever would be.

She came to a red light. Traffic and pedestrians were busy. She cleared her mind to concentrate, checking mirrors and surroundings. A car stopped behind her sat too close to her rear bumper. She hated tailgaters.

The light changed and she focused on driving, and how fast she could shower, dress, and get back to the bar. A couple of turns and then her street was straight ahead. A glance in the mirror showed her tailgater not far behind. Her shoulders tensed; HB's words imprinted on her brain. She turned down her street, and the vehicle followed. She kept on driving, past her house and turned onto the next street. The other car drove past.

She'd let herself get spooked. Wasn't the first time. She shrugged it off and made a U-turn.

Alanna had texted to say she and Max were taking Charlotte out for a movie and dinner and they'd be home after dark.

Once inside her home, she hurried to shower and dress.

***

HB paced in front of Rolin, who was busy behind the bar. "I'm going to head over there. It's not like her to be late, and she's not responding to calls."

"You're not going alone," said Rolin as he took payment from a customer. "I'll get Colleen to cover here, in the meantime try giving the Sergeant a call."

"On it," said HB, pressing the screen on his phone. "Sergeant, HB here. We might have a situation."

"Explain."

"Dorothy left here — Maxwell's — over 3 hours ago, heading home for an hour, and then was supposed to be back here 2 hours ago. We've heard nothing from her and that's not like her. Rolin and I are going to go over to her place after I hang up."

"Hold tight for a second, HB. You know officially my hands are tied. There's no criminal activity to warrant sending a patrol car. But I think you should trust your instincts. One more thing. Evidence bagged at the kidnap apartment has yielded something interesting. We found one of your business cards, with fingerprints belonging to a Miranda Porter — name mean anything to you?"

"Coming up empty. I've handed out a lot of cards. Who is she?"

"She's not on our radar. Only reason we have her prints is because she was charged with shoplifting as a teenager, but charges were dropped." Dead air for a few seconds before Keleher continued. "And before you ask, no, there's nothing new on Michelson. We found the boat belonging to Steve Kinney and located him as well. No joy. Both he and the boat have been participating in sailing events out of state, and only returned yesterday. Solid alibi."

"Damn. Another dead end. Thanks for the update. I'll be in touch when we know Dorothy's okay."

"If there is any trouble, it's 9-1-1 first. Got it? Then call me."

HB disconnected the call and turned to Rolin. "Let's go. I'll fill you in on the way."

A few minutes later HB pulled up near Dorothy's house. "Her Jeep is here ... Why isn't she answering?" HB was ready to jump from the car, but Rolin laid a hand on his arm.

"Let's take a second here. I'm not an investigator, but maybe we need to be careful. I know you're thinking

Michelson, but it could be she's having a nap, or lost track of time … There's no sign of Max's car; maybe she's with him?"

HB snorted. "Yeah, right. You don't even believe those words yourself, do you?"

Rolin frowned, and HB recalled Charlotte's assessment of the relationship between Rolin and Dorothy. She'd probably nailed it. Which meant keeping Dorothy safe was more important than ever.

"Let me try her home phone again," said Rolin. He put it on speaker, and both heard it go to voicemail. "Dee," said Rolin, "wondering where you are? We expected you here at the bar a couple of hours ago – please call."

"That's good," said HB. "Let me call Max on the off chance he knows anything." But Max's phone went unanswered as well, leaving HB the only option to leave a brief message. "Max, by chance is Dorothy with you. We, ah, can't seem to find her. Call me."

"He's not stupid, HB. Soon as he gets the message he'll be in touch, or race back here."

HB pointed. "The curtain just moved. Someone's inside."

CHAPTER THIRTY-FOUR

Dorothy listened to the answering machine as yet another call came in. This time it was Rolin looking for her. She could only hope he or HB would connect the dots and realize she was in trouble. The agitated young girl — she estimated her to be in her early twenties — who had barged into her home with Xander, risked a peek out the front window. Dorothy strained against the rope binding her wrists behind her, but she couldn't see out the window. Her worry was for Max, Alanna, and Charlotte. They'd walk into this trap if Dorothy couldn't get out of it first. She didn't have a lot of options, especially with her ankles tied to the legs of the dining room chair.

She was outnumbered, and Xander had the gun. She needed to stay focused and keep calm. But after listening to Xander's rant for the last hour, she didn't have much patience left.

And then he was in her face again. "This is all your fault. I only want Charlotte. Where is she?"

Dorothy shrugged her aching shoulders. How was she supposed to answer with her mouth taped. She flinched when he raised the gun over her head and waited for it to hit.

"Xander, stop! She doesn't know. We should just go."

He whirled around and advanced on the unnamed young woman. "Shut your mouth, or you'll be next."

Dorothy tried to make eye contact with her. Xander's companion didn't seem too sure of herself, as if she was in something way over her head. If only Dorothy could make a connection, she might be able to recruit her as an ally. She must see that Xander was losing it.

Xander flopped into a chair where he could watch both of them. "You just keep watching that window for anyone coming here."

"I'm getting hungry – how much longer are we gonna be here?"

Xander turned to Dorothy. "If I take the tape off, no screaming. Or I use this. Got it?"

Nodding, she tried not to react as the tape was torn away from her mouth. She licked her lips, tasting blood where the skin ripped off. Her voice came out as a whisper. "Could I have some water?"

"Tell her," he pointed to his accomplice, "what she can find to eat in the kitchen. She'll bring back water."

Dorothy locked eyes with her. "In the fridge, there's leftovers. Or cold meat to make a sandwich."

The girl moved away, and Dorothy focused on Xander. "So, Olivia wasn't involved in the kidnapping after all. You must have been planning this for a long time. So many details."

"She was useful for a while and I needed to keep her interested, in me. But it didn't play out the way I wanted. I decided not to involve her." Xander grunted. "You have no idea the energy she took from me. No wish to be saddled with her for any length of time."

"And Frisco Butler – he wasn't really involved either, right." Dorothy kept playing for time. "You know we found a piece of your torn boxing glove on his body?"

"Drug addled patsy. When I asked him to sell my gloves — for a cut of course, we met so I could show them to him. So easy to set up the drug angle too, with Mandy's help. Greed gets them every time."

Of course, Mandy Peterson whom HB had assessed as odd. Dorothy decided not to comment on the irony. "So, that's your friend's name. I take it she's been in on this from the start?"

Xander opened his mouth and stopped. "Shut up! What was that noise? Someone's here!" He waved the gun in her face.

Dorothy recognized the sound. It was the door between her home and her father's apartment. There was a crash in the kitchen and then silence.

Xander ran toward the sound as the front door burst open and HB rushed in. "Hold it right there," shouted Xander. "Get over next to her and keep your hands where I can see them."

The expression on HB's face silenced Dorothy.

"Mandy!" Xander shouted. "Get in here." He moved a few steps toward the kitchen.

Dorothy looked at HB, who muttered. "I didn't see that coming. You okay?"

She nodded, and noted with satisfaction Xander was now in a quandary as he yo-yoed between the kitchen and then back to her location, several times. Leave the room, with HB unrestrained, to find Mandy, or stay put. "Mandy! Answer me dammit."

His face beaded with sweat and his eyes darted back and forth. Finally, he pointed the gun at HB. "Come with me — don't try anything — I know how to use this."

HB raised his hands. "You need to relax. I won't do anything."

While Xander had been distracted over Mandy, HB had managed to loosen the rope on Dorothy's wrists. When they left her sight, she worked at the binding feverishly and felt it give way. She quickly untied her ankles. Before she could stand, HB led the way back into the room. Behind him was Mandy, and Rolin! Bringing up the rear was Xander, gun pressed up against Rolin's back.

So much could go wrong — Dorothy bit down on her rising panic. Xander hadn't noticed she was free, but HB had. He allowed Xander to think he was still in charge as he motioned HB next to Dorothy, and Rolin to the other side.

Mandy held a ball of kitchen twine, as if that would hold either of the men.

Xander had to know the odds weren't in his favor, but his erratic behavior meant all bets were off. He moved in closer to instruct Mandy in using the twine on Rolin.

Dorothy seized the moment and brought her arms up to knock the gun from Xander's hand. A shot rang out and the thud of a body hitting the floor was one Dorothy would never forget.

But then she was in Rolin's arms, his mouth on hers. A moment she wanted to last, but the sirens in the distance told her otherwise.

They pulled apart and for a moment there was no one else in the room except for her and Rolin. An anguished moan rocketed her back to reality.

Xander Michelson writhed on the floor, clutching his shoulder. Mandy Peterson sat next to him cradling his head in her lap, sobbing. His gun not close enough to reach.

HB. She turned to him as he returned his gun to his ankle holster. "Michelson never searched me. What can I say?"

Dorothy gave HB a hug. "I can say – well done!"

Rolin pulled her back close to him again and his concerned eyes searched her face. "Are you alright?"

She smiled at him, her heart about to burst. "I am now."

CHAPTER THIRTY-FIVE

HB had agreed to Shelby Keleher's request to unofficially review events in the informal setting of a local diner. He'd been up since before dawn, piecing together one last evaluation on this case for Dorothy, and now it was almost noon.

Shelby had just come from the courthouse. Xander Michelson, ironically, had been kept overnight in the same hospital as Etienne Rivard, but was stable enough to face booking and arraignment first thing in the morning.

He faced a litany of charges - ranging from theft of a firearm with intent to use, kidnap and extortion, to murder. "Don't think any lawyer will get him off that easy, Shelby. He's going to be out of the picture for a long, long time."

"At least he has legal counsel. Now he's been arraigned, with no bail of course, he's been carted off to enjoy a stay at the Multnomah County Detention Center."

"Could be a while before he comes to trial - I'll be sure to get tickets."

Shelby's unexpected giggle was brief, causing HB a ripple of pride that he made her laugh. Then she grew serious.

"I'm impressed with you HB, and of course Dorothy. I haven't touched base with her today, but I hope she's recovered from her ordeal at the hands of Xander Michelson. I don't advocate the use of firearms by civilians, but you reacted professionally to prevent a scenario outcome that could have been nasty."

Praise never sat well with him, and he responded gruffly. "Not one of my favorite things to do but it's what I get paid for.

Anyway, yes Dorothy is fine. We've been through a lot over the years. Having each other's back is second nature. When I saw her trussed up ..."

"But how did Rolin get in? No one has explained it to me yet."

HB was relieved to be on more neutral ground. "I had a key and gave it to him. Boss —Dorothy — always wants me to have one for, well, for situations like this. And he called 9-1-1 before he tackled Mandy."

"Makes sense." Shelby motioned the server for a refill. "Coffee's not bad here. Better than the station rubbish."

"Mine's better," replied HB. "You can be the judge sometime."

"I'm sure it is" She paused while their cups were refilled. "Look, I'd like to revisit a few things before I close this case. Mandy Peterson."

"AKA Miranda Porter. Wondered when you'd get around to asking about her."

Shelby frowned and over-stirred her coffee. "We didn't have enough time to connect the dots, and you wouldn't be wrong to say we dropped the ball on this."

HB couldn't meet Shelby's eyes and mumbled. "Can't win them all. I did have my doubts about her but she's a good actress. Maybe she took lessons from Olivia. Speaking of, what's going to happen to her? She's a witness, right? But no charges. Unless you know something I don't."

"Olivia. I'll get to her in a minute. First this." Shelby reached beside her and brought a folder to the table. "Here, this might explain. It came in late last night."

HB opened the file and scanned the information. "Ah, there you go." He saw a mug shot of Miranda Porter, age 17. "Different hair color, and I bet she's a hundred pounds heavier in this shot. Even if we'd had this, I'm not sure I'd have recognized her as Mandy Peterson."

"Timing was off getting the info. But better late than never. She's now been charged under her real name, as an accessory to kidnap and extortion. Using Mandy Peterson on her resume with the winery helped her get the job. Unless there's some kind of deal with the DA's office, she's looking at some serious time as well. She's providing information on the whole kidnap scheme to help herself."

She returned the file to her side. "Foolish girl, getting mixed up with Xander Michelson. On to better subjects, then," said Shelby. "What's the word on Etienne. Getting stronger I hope?"

HB pushed his empty cup to one side. "I called the hospital earlier and he is improved big time. Knowing Xander's been caught is helping his recovery. Max and Alanna are taking Charlotte to see him."

"Very glad to hear it. He's been through enough. He and Charlotte deserve to have a good outcome from all of this." Shelby stood. "I need to be getting on with my day, but ..."

"But?" asked HB. "And you were going to say something about Olivia."

She partially pulled a document from her shoulder bag. "I have a present for her, which I'm going to personally deliver. Interested in coming along? I can rescind my directive that she not leave town but will need to be assured we can reach her."

HB eyed the familiar looking document and couldn't help smiling. "Wouldn't want to miss this. Love to come along."

"Good. While there I need a word with the person in charge ..."

"I believe it's Tom Romano in charge until Etienne is ready to take back the reins. I wonder if he knows Mandy will have to be replaced."

"Yes, Tom Romano. Let's go, you can ride with me."

On the way to the winery, HB received a text and relayed the news to Shelby. "From Charlotte. Etienne is doing so well, he's being discharged today she wants me to come and get them and bring him home." He replied to Charlotte she should tell Max and Alanna they could leave, and he'd be there later.

"That's good news," she said. "I won't keep you here any longer than necessary."

Arriving at the vineyards they saw a sign erected at the front gates.

Welcome Home Etienne

Shelby smiled. "That's a nice touch. I'll be glad when he's back in charge. His Pinot Noir is one of my favorites."

"Agreed. Dorothy says it's one of their best sellers at Maxwell's."

As they parked in front of the house, HB heard another vehicle approaching. He turned and recognized an airport cab. He nudged Shelby as she knocked on the door. "We may have arrived none too soon."

Olivia St John-Rivard opened the door, but her face fell when she recognized her callers. "What do you want?"

"Ms. St John-Rivard - going somewhere?" Shelby's voice was cold and professional. HB stood by and watched the play of expressions across Olivia's face. "Were you not told to stay in town? Or are you heading to a local hotel?"

HB peeked around Shelby and saw an expensive set of luggage standing behind Olivia. Busted!

"I ... I was just about to call and leave you a message. Not that ..."

Shelby cut her off. "Don't want to hear it. Here, I have something for you." She held the document up in front of Olivia's face.

As her eyes took in the instructions on the restraining order, she paled, and then her brand of righteous anger rose to the surface. "How dare he! Charlotte is still my daughter, too. He can't stop me from seeing her! I'll get my lawyer on this right away!"

"Yes, you just do that, Ms. St John. In the meantime, stay away from your daughter and her father, and this property."

HB smirked at Shelby's deliberate use of Olivia's maiden name.

The cab driver honked his horn; HB turned and shouted, "Five minutes, pal."

Shelby pulled out her notebook. "I'll save you the call to my office. You can tell me here and now, where I can always reach you. And believe me, if I find I can't reach you, it won't go well for you."

Olivia pursed her lips and her eyes flashed. "Fine. Use my cell number. I ... I'm not quite sure where I'll be staying. Somewhere in Texas I hope."

Shelby verified the cell number and snapped her notebook shut. "Thank you. You are free to go. Have a nice day."

HB couldn't resist a tip of his hat at Olivia, turned and followed Shelby back down the steps.

As they walked toward the bottling area, HB laughed. "Oh, man. The look on her face was priceless. She met her match with you."

"Let's just say I'm no fan of entitled money arrogance. Anytime I can even the score, is a good day for me. Now, let's find Tom Romano and give him some good news."

Heavy dark clouds had moved in and as rain began to fall, they ran the last few steps to the building. As they shook off their jackets, an authoritative voice met them.

"Sorry, we're not open yet."

"Tom Romano?" Shelby addressed the foreman of the winery. "You will be glad to know Mr. Rivard is being discharged today and will be home with Charlotte later."

Romano's face broke into a smile of relief. "About time we had some good news. Thank you. And can I ask if I saw the bit ... I mean Ms. St John-Rivard getting into a cab? Is she gone?"

HB confirmed Romano was right. "I know I'm glad she's gone, and I don't work here."

Romano laughed. "Man, you have no idea - oh then again, maybe you do."

Shelby broke in. "Are you aware we also have Mandy Peterson under arrest? You'll be short an employee."

"Mandy? What the hell? She called in sick yesterday, but you're saying she was involved in all this?"

"I can't really comment, Mr. Romano, but no doubt you'll soon hear more details on the evening news, or from Mr. Rivard himself when he returns. A word of advice though, he probably won't be up to much work involvement for a while."

"No worries, Sergeant. All under control. I'll be sending someone into the house to do a clean-up, to get it ready for their return. They have been missed." He smiled at them, "Even Charlotte!"

"I'm sure your efforts will be appreciated," said Shelby. "We'll leave you to it."

"Oh, hang on, before you go." Tom Romano moved over to a wine-sampling table and brought out two bottles of their best Pinot Noir. "Thank you both for bringing this to a better conclusion than many of us expected. Please accept these and enjoy."

Shelby held up a hand. "Thank you, but it's against department regulations for me to accept any kind of gift. Perhaps Mr. Bartholomew would be happy with both?"

HB took the bottles. "Who am I to argue with the police?"

They thanked him and returned to her car.

As they drove away from the winery, Shelby commented. "I'm getting used to your company HB." She eyed the bottles sitting in his lap. "I like the perks you get on this job of yours. Would love to pick your brain sometime on how you handle your investigations."

HB laughed. "That might cost you. Can you afford me?"

She laughed out loud. "Are you sure you don't want to join the police force?"

Grinning, HB retorted. "No way. I don't look good in a uniform."

After leaving the winery, Shelby dropped HB off near his car. "Oh, and one thing before you go. You can pass this on to Dorothy as well. Reg Pierson has taken early retirement and

I've been asked to stay on as his replacement. So, we might be working together again."

CHAPTER THIRTY-SIX

"Mr. Rivard – make sure you follow these after care instructions. Or should I give your daughter the responsibility?" The hospital nurse held Etienne Rivard's discharge papers in her hand. "And yes, you are required to sit in this wheelchair until you leave the building."

HB had his hands on the back of the wheelchair, ready to propel Etienne on his journey home. Charlotte insisted he be the one to drive her father back to their house. Taking care of him until he was fully recovered might cramp her angry-at-the-world personality, but he noted changes already. The black nail polish and raccoon-rimmed eyes were cleaned up. Most of the unnatural color had gone from her hair and only one small nose piercing remained. Progress, or temporary image?

She grasped a bouquet of get-well balloons and Etienne balanced a box of greeting cards on his lap. They were ready.

Etienne tried to twist his head to see HB. "I hope this isn't an inconvenience, Mr. Bartholomew, and I apologize if Charlotte has overstepped her – ah – authority."

"You can call me HB. I think I learned a few days ago not to resist Hurricane Charlotte."

Etienne laughed. "She can be a force to be reckoned with. I ... I owe her a lot. And," he tapped his daughter's arm, "I think we should start with ordering in pizza, or Pad Thai, for dinner? The invitation includes HB of course."

"Dad, Uncle Max took me for groceries. And Aunt Alanna helped me make lasagna! You will come, right, HB?"

"I may have to take a rain check," he began and then stopped at the crestfallen look on her face. "It depends on the time. I have a – meeting – later this evening I need to go to."

"We can eat early; Dad shouldn't have a late night anyway. Then you can leave for your meeting. Please?"

"I think you've lost this one, HB."

They drove back to the winery estate, Charlotte going a mile a minute about cleaning the house and trips they could have, and how she'd maybe like to help at the winery. "That doesn't mean I've changed my mind about being a private investigator!"

HB smiled and made no comment. Experience had taught him life often had other plans, but he wouldn't be the one to put a damper on her dreams. He could hear her tapping away on her phone as she sat in the back seat. Etienne, beside him, was quiet. HB glanced at him. His eyes were closed, but his face was relaxed. Worry lines from days in the hospital were gone. Getting him home appeared to be good medicine.

They pulled into the long drive leading up to the main house. HB clued in to what Charlotte had been doing – a heads up to the staff they were arriving. Workers lined the parking area and a banner proclaimed, Welcome Home, Etienne.

Charlotte reached over the seat and tapped her father on his shoulder. "See, Dad, they know you're the best, too!"

***

"And here's the man of the hour!"

A round of applause, led by Max, greeted HB as he walked into Maxwell's at 7.00. The senior Dennehy waved him over to their table, joining Alanna and Dorothy.

"Hope you've left room for a special dinner? And, here comes Rolin," she said, her heart skipping a beat as he drew near to her. She suddenly felt awkward, they hadn't had any time to talk about *the kiss*. He smiled at her. A smile she'd seen hundreds of times, yet now it was new, different somehow. She shook her head. She needed to concentrate and pushed away the tingle of excitement his presence had ignited.

Jordan Klein was also at the table. The newest employee on Dorothy's team beamed with pride at being included.

"First round's on the house," said Rolin, as Colleen approached to take their orders.

"Etienne Rivard is now home and settled?" asked Dorothy.

"He is," laughed HB. "Although I think Charlotte's care of him might get old real fast." He turned to Alanna. "I believe you're responsible for the delicious lasagna I enjoyed?"

Alanna smiled. "That girl only needs adults to listen — truly listen — to her. She loves her dad and wants to make up for her past behavior with him. I sent her home with a couple of cookbooks. From what she told me, her mother didn't spend a lot of time in the kitchen. So, she's eager to learn. Max has offered her some cooking lessons as well. I'd say we haven't seen the last of her."

Dorothy reached over and laid a hand on HB's wrist. "This case brought out a side to you none of us have seen. I know I could never have built the bond you've got with her. Well done." And then understanding her friend's unease at being the center of attention she turned to Jordan.

"Jordan Klein. We should have an award for most improved employee. You had a rough start with Quail Investigations, but you've proved yourself. And if HB agrees, I believe we can waive the remainder of your probation period."

"Really? Wow. I mean, thank you. I've learned a lot working with HB. You can count on me!"

Their meals began to arrive, and Dorothy took a moment to consider the faces around her table. When her gaze landed on Rolin, she was surprised to see him watching her. There was that smile again, and for a moment the other faces disappeared. He raised his glass in a quiet toast toward her. Contentment mixed with anticipation, and she prayed she didn't have an insipid grin on her face. She found her glass and acknowledged him, then pulled her gaze away and focused on the conversation all around her.

"An Alaskan cruise? I had a friend who did one a few years back. Said it was the most amazing thing he'd done." Jordan had a sociable streak and could hold his own in any of the conversations, but Dorothy knew he might have to tame that talent in surveillance. Still, she was pleased at how well he fit in, and HB appeared to like working with him as well. All was good.

Max leaned over to brush Alanna's cheek with a kiss. "We have a few months to plan all the details, don't we, darlin?"

"Least of which is packing remedies for seasickness. I've no idea what kind of sea-legs you have, my love."

Eventually the table was cleared of empty plates and conversation had lulled in response to full stomachs. Max stifled a yawn. "Sorry, folks, but I think it's time Alanna and I called it a night. It's been a rough couple of weeks, and I think you all deserve a night off."

"The night's still young, Max," said Rolin. "You leave now you don't know what you might be missing."

Max offered a sage smile in Rolin's direction. "Exactly why we are leaving. I'm long past wanting to see what Friday night excitement might bring. I've had my share."

Dorothy stood to give her dad a kiss and then hugged Alanna. "Straight home, right?"

She watched them leave. There were still a lot of full tables, but younger ones would be heading for the night life downtown before long. Almost as she thought it, Jordan stood.

"Thanks so much for the dinner, Ms. Dennehy. Um, if you don't mind, I said I'd try and meet some friends. Friday night, you know."

"Just be in shape to work come Monday morning. HB's told me there are a couple of new clients on deck for next week."

"I'll be ready. Goodnight."

"So, HB," said Rolin as the door closed behind Jordan, "your young protégé is measuring up to expectations?"

"He has potential. Thinks fast. He's a good addition."

"And you're vindicated now in your hiring of him," laughed Dorothy. "Oh, reminds me. Rolin and I have decided to keep Maxwell's closed on Mondays. A trial run for now, but I have a feeling it will be permanent. So," she hesitated, "I can always lend a hand if need be."

"Very subtle, Dee. Admit it, this case made you realize what you've been missing."

"I may have been missing a lot of things," she said.

HB coughed. "And on that note, I'm calling it a night as well. Nice meal, thanks again, Boss."

"Enjoy your weekend, HB. You've earned the down time."

"Except for paperwork," HB groused good naturedly, then followed several couples out the door.

Rolin walked over and went behind the bar. He turned to face Dorothy, holding a bottle of their best bourbon. "Join me for a night cap, Miss?"

He stood there, expectantly. A look on his face kindled an intense wave of desire deep within her. Her chest tightened and she realized how much she wanted him. This couldn't be rushed.

"A nightcap? Do I know you well enough? What would my father say?"

Rolin smiled. "I believe your father might approve. I could call him?"

Dorothy laughed. "And you would, too, wouldn't you."

She followed him to his office, and he closed the door behind her. She wasn't sure, but she thought those two leather chairs might be sitting closer together than the last time she'd been in here. Almost face to face.

The lighting was subdued, and they sat. Rolin poured two glasses. "To us, Dee. Or am I mistaken? Things have changed – for the better?"

She sipped at the amber liquid. The warmth from the drink couldn't compete with the heat rising within her. She raised her eyes and got lost in the depth of emotion shown in his. Her hand trembled as she put the drink down. Her voice a whisper, "Rolin – I ... I think I've fallen in love with you."

He put his drink aside and leaned forward to cup her face in his strong hands. His voice caught and was husky. "Dee, I know this might be complicated – with our history. But I've never been more sure of anything than when I tell you this. I love you. And not as a friend." His voice caught. "You've no idea how much I want you right now."

She closed her eyes and let him kiss her. His lips were soft against hers and every nerve in her being came alive. She responded with an urgency that surprised her, pulling back when a moan threatened to escape. Her heart hammered and words would never be enough. But he knew, she could tell he *knew* what she was feeling. He reached for her hands, pulling her to her feet. And then she was embraced in those arms she'd longed to feel about her. Arms that would keep her safe, that would be hers alone. He pulled her tight, no mistaking his intent. But not here.

She brought her hands up to his chest and gently pushed away. "Do you still want to call my father?"

Rolin laughed, but it was a laugh laced with intimacy. To be shared solely with her. He traced the outline of her jaw and brought his fingers to rest against her lips. "I don't want to talk to anyone other than you."

"Right answer," she grew bolder and pulled him closer to her whispering in his ear, "Can we go upstairs – to talk?"

He kissed her forehead. "Yes."

There would be more cases to investigate, there would be crises to manage. But not now, not tonight.

Tonight belonged to them.

THE END

Acknowledgements for Cultivating the Truth

Once again, we extend our heartfelt thanks and gratitude to our wonderful Beta Readers. Their feedback and observations are golden to us. They are our silent partners in this process.

Thank you so much - Margret C, Gloria F, Shirley J, Laurie H, Linda M, and Wendy W.

Also by Jamie Tremain

The Dorothy Dennehy Mystery Series (best read in order)
The Silk Shroud
Lightning Strike
Beholden to None
Cultivating the Truth

The Grant's Crossing Series (best read in order)
Death on the Alder
Resort to Murder
Acting Off-Script

**The Mechanic Falls Gem Caper Series
(as Ferris Tremain – with Gloria Ferris)**
Worlds May Change
Tequila Claus – A Christmas Short

Other Series Information

Grant's Crossing Series (by Jamie Tremain)

Rural small-town Ontario is the setting for this light mystery series. Alysha Grant is the young, and inexperienced, new owner of Leven Lodge – a guest home for those more mature folks not yet ready for a nursing home. Inheriting the former family property, she depends on her staff's capable skills to help her as she grows into her new role.

Residents aren't always what they portray, many have secrets. Romance and matters of the heart are no strangers to any of them, but when crime affects Leven Lodge, Alysha doesn't hesitate to become involved.

Fans of small-town characters will enjoy getting to know the residents of Leven Lodge and Grant's Crossing. Add a sprinkling of romance and cozy elements and you'll want to keep coming back for more.

Mechanic Falls Gem Caper Series (by Ferris Tremain)

Tori Marsh fled to Mechanic Falls when she stole gems belonging to criminals. It was only meant to be a temporary hideout – until it was safe to move on.

But she stayed and has become part of Amberly and Willoughby Thwackbottom's lives. Identical twin morticians who kept Tori safe, and who are now her family.

When criminal elements are blended with quirky, but loveable characters, it leads to a caper-style, action-packed story. Especially when all the players have a Robin Hood sense of justice.

About the Authors

Pam Blance:

Reading and writing are passions for Pam. And in that order. She believes it's a necessity to do a whole lot of reading in order to write well. She grew up in Scotland, with a father who hammered away at an old manual typewriter producing poems and articles. Her writing bug is part of her DNA. After immigrating to Canada in the sixties, Pam worked in several different industries. Raising three children, with a full-time job, only left her time to scribble, mainly for herself.

In 2007, after attending writing workshops, she shared her aspirations with work colleague, Liz Lindsay. A writing partnership was born, and Jamie Tremain came to life. Long retired from the corporate jungle affords time to focus on writing. Having six published books is just the beginning – the best is yet to come!

Reach her at pamjblance@gmail.com

Liz Lindsay

"I'm not ignoring you; I'm plotting." Most days find Liz at her computer either typing like mad or staring off into space. Both are means to an end. She may be working on another collaborative Jamie Tremain story, preparing to send her latest contribution to Pam Blance, for her turn. Or, it might be to add another short story to her inventory. Fodder for a future collection to be published.

For almost twenty years, she and Pam have worked together as Jamie Tremain, producing two mystery series and a total of 6 books to date. Producing a monthly Jamie Tremain newsletter and staying up to date with fans means she'll probably need another new keyboard soon.

Along with Pam, Liz's recent new partnering with fellow Guelph author Gloria Ferris under the name Ferris Tremain has been a lot of fun. Lots of ideas for future escapades in Mechanic Falls. If two minds are better than one – imagine what three can do!

When not writing Liz enjoys British based detective series, noting what she finds intriguing and well-written – with the storylines and characters. Oh, and in quieter moments, it's back to plotting.

Reach her at lizlindsay528@yahoo.com

Don't miss out!

Visit the website below and you can sign up to receive emails whenever Jamie Tremain publishes a new book. There's no charge and no obligation.

https://books2read.com/r/B-A-VAAO-MPSPC

Connecting independent readers to independent writers.

Milton Keynes UK
Ingram Content Group UK Ltd.
UKHW010835071223
433828UK00001B/30